Tinker – Wireless Operator

By G. H. Teed

Illustrated by Stanley Rogers

First Published in the Union Jack magazine,
New Series, No. 1028, 23 June 1923.

Stillwoods Edition

Stillwoods.Blogspot.Ca

Catalogue Information:

Title: Tinker – Wireless Operator
Author: G. H. Teed (1886-1938)
Illustrated by: Stanley Rogers
First Published anonymously in the Union Jack magazine, New
    Series, No. 1028, 23 June 1923.
This Edition by: Stillwoods, 2023
ISBN Canada: 978-1-998819-22-5
Blog: Stillwoods.Blogspot.Ca
Author Blog: http://ghteed.blogspot.com/
Old Storefront: http://www.lulu.com/spotlight/lulubook22

https://tinyurl.com/ve25d42s This link should go to a spreadsheet of all known Teed stories. The list is annotated with various information on the stories and my progress with recapturing the work. The library of Teed's stories increases almost weekly. Check at Lulu.Com for the earlier publications. Search for Teed. /drf

Keywords: Sexton Blake, Tinker, Texas.

Cautionary Note: This series of books by Stillwoods are intended to make the stories of G. H. Teed, born in New Brunswick, Canada, available to collectors and researchers. The editor, or rather digitizer has not altered the original publication.

This story may contain language and racial terms that are not appropriate today. I apologize for them; I know that the author was using his voice to excite and entertain an adventurous English audience. These works were published from 82 to 110 years ago. Most every work has characters of redeeming ethnicity within.

I hope you enjoy and share these stories; I have.

Doug Frizzle

A Grand New Long Story of Adventure and Detective Work on Land and on the High Seas. Introducing SEXTON BLAKE, detective, and TINKER his assistant. Complete in this issue.

This story, written in the captivating style the creator of Mlle. Yvonne and other favourite U.J. characters knows how to put across, records a particularly interesting exploit of Tinker's. The scene is laid in London, shifts to Cardiff, and thence to the broad Atlantic, finishing up on the coast of Mexico. It is action all the way —action vividly described, gripping and convincing.

Please note that most of the supplementary content of this issue of the Union Jack magazine was not available.../drf

TINKER-WIRELESS OPERATOR!

This story, written in the captivating style the creator of Mlle. Yvonne and other favourite U.J. characters knows how to put across, records a particularly interesting exploit of Tinker's. The scene is laid in London, shifts to Cardiff, and thence to the broad Atlantic, finishing up on the coast of Mexico. It is action all the way—action vividly described, :: :: gripping and convincing. :: ::

THE FIRST CHAPTER.
Turned Down.

SEXTON BLAKE smiled patiently across at the little dark-skinned man who sat facing him in the consulting-room at Baker Street.

"Believe me, Senor Barbosa, I am sorry!" he said. "But, as I have told you on two previous occasions, it is impossible for me to assist you If it were within my power to do so I should at once tell you so. I believe all you have told me about this man, Pancho Morales, and it is clear that you have suffered grievously at his hands. But what can I do? You have no corroboration such as a court of law would require, and I do not see how I can possibly secure it for you.

"You. acknowledge, yourself, that Pancho Morales is in practical control of the whole district of Chihuahua—one of the most extensive in Mexico. Up to now the Mexican Government itself has failed to run him to earth, even though it has sent several large and well-equipped expeditions after him.

"He is master of all that part of the country—a country which I, from personal knowledge, know to be of a very wild and difficult nature. Therefore, you must see that, where several armies have failed, I should stand very little chance when playing what would practically be a lone hand. The best advice I can give you is to put this idea from your mind, for the present, at least. Later on, if circumstances should alter, I shall do what I can to help you."

The little Mexican pulled nervously at his straggling grey moustache and eyed Blake pleadingly.

It would have been difficult to believe that, less than two years before, this same man had been one of the wealthiest of the hacienda owners of Northern Mexico. But such had been the case, although, at the time of his visit to Sexton Blake, he had been reduced almost to beggary, owing, according to his story, to the bandit depredations of the notorious Pancho Morales, who, for five years on end, had kept that part of Mexico under a ruthless heel.

It was over a month since he had first come to Blake with a story which

THE FIRST CHAPTER.   *Turned Down.*

SEXTON BLAKE smiled patiently across at the little dark-skinned man who sat facing him in the consulting-room at Baker Street.

"Believe me, Senor Barbosa, I am sorry!" he said. "But, as I have told you on two previous occasions, it is impossible for me to assist you. If it were within my power to do so I should at once tell you so. I believe all you have told me about this man, Pancho Morales, and it is clear that you have suffered grievously at his hands. But what can I do? You have no corroboration such as a court of law would require, and I do not see how I can possibly secure it for you.

"You acknowledge, yourself, that Pancho Morales is in practical control of the whole district of Chihuahua —one of the most extensive in Mexico. Up to now the Mexican Government itself has failed to run him to earth, even though it has sent several large and well-equipped expeditions after him.

"He is master of all that part of the country —a country which I, from personal knowledge, know to be of a very wild and difficult nature. Therefore, you must see that, where several armies have failed, I should stand very little chance when playing what would practically be a lone hand. The best advice I can give you is to put this idea from your mind, for the present, at least. Later on, if circumstances should alter, I shall do what I can to help you."

The little Mexican pulled nervously at his straggling grey moustache and eyed Blake pleadingly.

It would have been difficult to believe that, less than two years before, this same man had been one of the wealthiest, of the hacienda owners of Northern Mexico. But such had been the case, although, at the time of his visit to Sexton Blake, he had been reduced almost to beggary, owing, according to his story, to the bandit depredations of the notorious Pancho Morales, who, for five years on end, had kept that part of Mexico under a ruthless heel.

It was over a month since he had first come to Blake with a story which had stirred the detective's sympathy deeply. It seemed that for some three years Morales had preyed on Barbosa's hacienda, and, during that time, had practically fed his rabble by drawing on Barbosa's vast herds of cattle.

But such wholesale looting could not go on for ever, and when at last the cattle had given out, he had made demands for money. More than once Barbosa had tried to escape from the district, for he was loyal to the Government, but Morales kept too close a watch on him for that to succeed. Perforce, he had to yield to the outlaw's demands, until when his money had gone, even as his cattle, he was compelled to sacrifice next his jewels and family possessions.

If it had been possible to find a buyer for his hacienda, Morales would have forced him to sell that as well, but no one wanted to invest money in a district where even a pretence of security did not exist.

It would seem that Morales might have stopped at that; but he had not. Spurred on by the form of devastating hatred which certain curious natures feel against those whom they have wronged, Pancho Morales cast about for still other means by which he could injure Barbosa. And it was then his eagle eye fell upon Barbosa's only child, a girl of seventeen years of age, whose soft Spanish eyes were just beginning to peep into the strange vista of coming womanhood.

On a wild night, when a hurricane was sweeping across the country, Morales had appeared at the hacienda with a body of his riders, and had abducted the girl. Barbosa, despite his age and broken spirit, had put up a strenuous resistance without avail.

He had been hurled over the corral-fence while the riders had ridden off, his last conscious recollection being Morales' jeers that he hoped he would find some compensation in knowing that he was to become the father-in-law of Pancho Morales.

Utterly ruined and completely broken, Barbosa had succeeded at last in escaping. He had made his way to Mexico City, where he had sought the aid of the Government to which he had been faithful so long.

He had been rewarded with a good deal of sympathy, and a punitive expedition had eventually been sent into Chihuahua to try and lay Morales by the heels. But the bandit, secure in his retreat among the hills, had only laughed, the while his followers kept up a continual harrying of the column until it was forced to retreat.

An Englishman in Mexico City, who had heard Barbosa's story, had made the suggestion that, where force was useless, strategy might be employed, and he had followed this up by saying that, if any man living was capable of outwitting Pancho Morales, that man was Sexton Blake, the London criminologist. Friends had subscribed enough to send Barbosa to London, and to keep him in modest lodgings for a time.

As soon as he had reached England he had at once called upon Blake and had laid his case before him. But, while he sympathised with the old man, Sexton Blake could not see any real prospect of success in trying to penetrate into the wilds of Chihuahua after Morales.

Not that he considered the feat an impossibility —Blake never called anything an impossibility until he had proven it to be so. But such an attempt, he knew, would demand a period for its execution which his present engagements would not permit him to give.

He had explained this to Senor Barbosa at the time of the latter's, first visit, but the little Mexican had returned again and yet again. And now, on this final occasion, he had made a very eloquent plea which it hurt Blake to turn down, but which he knew he must. Hence the words which have been quoted above, and which Blake softened by a kindly smile.

"That, then, is final, senor?"

"I am sorry, but it is!"

"Then, if you refuse to assist me, Senor Blake, it means that I must return to Mexico and live alone with my unhappy memories. Until even to-day I had hoped against hope that you would listen to my plea."

"Believe me, senor, I would help you if I could. But surely you see how I am placed. I have other clients whose affairs are quite as pressing as yours. Could I, in honour to the undertakings I have given, them, go out to Mexico on what might well prove a very long chase? If I could see any possible chance of getting hold of this man, Pancho Morales, within a short time —if, for example, he were in Mexico City, then I should not hesitate. I should go at once and lay him by the heels. But, under existing circumstances —no."

The Mexican rose with a heavy sigh.

"It is as you say, Senor Blake. I cannot but acknowledge the justice of your words. In trouble we are all of us prone to be selfish, I fear. I thank you, senor, for having listened to me so patiently on my various visits here. Adios, senor."

With that he held out his hand, which Blake took with a few more sympathetic words. Then Blake courteously accompanied the old man to the door. On his return to the consulting-room, he found Tinker standing at the window watching the Mexican make his way slowly along Baker Street.

"It is jolly tough on the old boy, guv'nor," he said. "It's a pity this bird Morales isn't where we could get at him!"

"I would do more than strain a point if it were in any way feasible, my lad," responded Blake. "But it isn't, so it is no use discussing the matter further. I feel very sorry indeed for Senor Barbosa, but it is kinder to let him know, once and for all, that his request is an impossible one. Now, sit down, and let us get these papers finished off. We are due at the Venetia at one o'clock, and it is past twelve already."

They worked away steadily until a quarter to one, when Blake pushed aside the last document and rose. While he made his way along to the dressing-room to slip into another suit, Tinker got his motoring-coat and cap.

A few minutes later, with the lad at the wheel of the Grey Panther, they were on their way to the Venetia, where they were to lunch in the grill with Gordon Lindsay, Blake's Montreal correspondent, who had arrived in England the previous evening on a special mission.

Tinker drove by way of Oxford Street and Regent Street, but although the Venetia had an entrance in Oxford Street as well as in Piccadilly, they did not draw up there as he knew the conditions for parking the car were better in Piccadilly than on the other side. Therefore he rounded the corner and drew slowly along until he reached the kerb in front of the hotel.

Blake climbed out while Tinker turned the car into the parking line in the middle of the street; then he shut off the engine and ran across to join Blake, who was standing talking with Kelly, the commissionaire, while he waited for the lad.

He gave Kelly a friendly nod as he followed Blake into the lobby, but scarcely had Tinker stepped inside than he gave vent to a startled "ouch," as Blake was sent careening back upon him by two porters, who were dragging a shouting, and apparently very excited, man from the lounge to the street.

Being behind Blake, Tinker could not at first see just what was taking place, but, as he got his foot clear, he stepped to one side and saw with amazement that the recalcitrant one was none other than Senor Barbosa, the little Mexican, who had called upon Blake only an hour or so before.

Blake, in the meantime, had laid a hand none too gently on the shoulder of one of the porters, thrusting him aside and bringing him face to face with the Mexican. The latter, who had been shouting unintelligible Spanish at the top of his lungs, paused as he recognised Blake; the next instant he hurled himself forward, almost embracing Blake in the act.

"Senor —Senor Blake," he cried; "it is that I am being insulted! I have seen him —I have spoken to him, but the evil one did but laugh at me and spit in my face! Then, after that unforgivable insult I did strike him, and now I am insulted! Tell them who I am, senor, and then take me back into the hotel, where I will show you the evil one and you can deal with him. The cursed mestizo to dare to flaunt his evil so openly —to think —"

Blake held up his hand.

"Just a moment, senor," he said quietly. "We cannot talk here, for we are blocking the way." Then to the two porters. "Leave this gentleman alone. He is known to me, and I will vouch for him. Come over here, Senor Barbosa?"

As the Mexican turned to follow, one of the porters, who apparently chose to misunderstand Blake, put out his hand; but it never reached the little Mexican. Kelly, who had appeared on the scene in time to hear the latter part of Blake's remarks, shot out his huge hand and grabbed the porter by the neck.

"Ye'll do that, will ye!" he growled. "Faith, and ye'll be asking for a quick journey into the gutter, me lad. An' didn't ye hear what Mr. Blake said to ye? When that gintleman speaks to ye, me lad, ye hump yerself, or it's Pat Kelly will paste yer ugly face for ye. Now, hump it, the pair of ye, and if any wan asks ye who sent ye, tell them it was the same Pat Kelly."

With that the giant commissionaire gave the porter a push that sent him flying into the lounge, followed by his mate, just as Kelly's hand went out a second time. Tinker had waited to witness the little incident, then, as Kelly winked solemnly at him, he gave a grin and moved off to the side of the lobby where Blake and Senor Barbosa were standing. Tinker was not a little curious to know what had led up to the trouble, and he was just in time to hear Blake saying:

"It is quite useless to go at things in such a way, senor. So far, I have only been able to gather that you have had some sort of trouble with a man in the hotel. Tell me just what has occurred, and I will see what I can do for you."

"But I have told you, Senor Blake, that it is he, the evil one!"

Blake smiled patiently.

"There are a lot of 'evil ones' in the world, senor. Just whom do you mean?"

"Why I have said, senor —it is Pancho Morales!"

"Ah!"

Blake stiffened as he heard the name. He was on the point of putting a further question, when the Mexican gave a jump and pointed excitedly over Blake's shoulder. "There he is —there he is!" he stuttered, his passion rising again.

Blake and Tinker both turned to regard the man whose attention had been attracted by Barbosa's cry. They saw a big florid man of dark skin and heavy black moustache, dressed very flashily in a morning coat of extreme cut and wearing an incongruous-looking wide-brimmed soft felt hat.

At the moment, he was standing, still smiling unabashed at his little compatriot, but it was only his lips that were smiling; his eyes were as hard and as cold as chilled steel. Thus for a moment; then he gave a shrug and passed out to the street. Senor Barbosa would have made after him, but Blake forcibly restrained him.

"Wait!" he ordered curtly. "Am I to understand that the man who has just passed out is the same Pancho Morales, the bandit of Chihuahua, who ruined you?"

"But yes, senor," wailed the other. "I have already told you."

"How did you know he was here at this hotel?"

"I was passing when I saw him get out of a cab and enter. I followed at once, and told him that I would appeal to the authorities."

"That was a mistake. The authorities can do nothing. Even if your own Government had made a complaint, which, under the present relations between Britain and Mexico, they could not do, I doubt if the authorities here could take any action. The whole world knows Morales is a bandit, but, don't forget, senor, he claims to possess just as much constitutional authority as the Government in Mexico City. But what does interest me is to find that he is in London. Where a man such as Pancho Morales is, then there is some very strong reason for his being there."

"He is, of course, up to some of his evil work. I know that man, I tell you. It would only be some very urgent matter that would bring him out of his Mexican hills."

"Possibly you are right. On the other hand, like other revolutionists whom I have known, he may have taken what boodle he could gather together and cleared out while it was possible. However, we certainly can't continue to discuss a matter of this sort in the lobby, senor. I have a lunch appointment in the grill-room, here. If you will join us, we can talk the matter over there."

The Mexican allowed himself to be urged into the lounge by Blake, and while they stood there they saw Gordon Lindsay coming towards them. When he had greeted Blake and Tinker, Blake presented Senor Barbosa, adding that he had taken the liberty of bringing him along as a guest. Lindsay, of course, accepted the addition with an expression of pleasure; then all four moved towards the wide, shallow steps which led down to the grill.

But as the others descended Blake muttered a word of excuse, saying that he would join them in a few minutes. He then went along to the private office of Browning, the manager of the hotel, whom he found busily at work as usual.

"I won't take but a few moments," said Blake, when they had shaken hands. "I want you to put through an inquiry for me, if you will be so good."

"Certainly —anything in my power. What is it?"

"I have reason to believe you have a Mexican staying here at the hotel —a big, flashily-dressed man who is wearing, to-day, a morning coat and a soft felt hat. His real name is Morales, but, of course he may be using another one at present. I want to know, whatever you can tell me about him —how long he has been here; if he is alone; when he is expected to leave, and so on. I am lunching in the grill, and will be there for about an hour."

"I shall make the inquiry at once," responded Browning. "I shall come down to the grill myself and tell you what I am able to discover."

Blake and Tinker stepped back as two porters came out, dragging a shouting and apparently very excited man. The detective saw with amazement that the recalcitrant one was none other than the Mexican who had called on him an hour or two before. (*Chapter 1.*)

ON rejoining his companions in the grill-room, Blake gave Gordon Lindsay a brief sketch of Senor Barbosa's troubles, which had culminated in the scene that he and Tinker had accidentally been mixed up in.

"I have put through an inquiry," he said, turning to the Mexican when he had finished. "When we have received the result of that we will talk the matter over. But until we have that it will not serve any good purpose to continue the discussion."

So, perforce, the still excited little man had to desist.

They had hardly begun the first course when Browning put in an appearance. Blake rose and joined him, and the two talked together for some minutes. Then Browning took himself off, and Blake reseated himself, but said nothing of what the manager had communicated to him.

Nor did he do so until the lunch was over and coffee had been served. Then, when the cigars had been passed round, Blake turned again to the Mexican.

"I have found out a few things concerning Morales, senor. He is, as we thought, staying here in the hotel, but not under his own name. He is registered as Pancho Fernandez. But that is of little importance. He has been here for about ten days, and has expressed his intention at the reception-desk of leaving to-morrow. And that is of importance to us.

"Now, I promised you, senor, that if it should occur that we could lure Morales in from his Chihuahuan hills, even as far as Mexico City, I would do what I could to help you. Instead of in Mexico City we have him here —right under our noses, so to say —in London. But that by no means places him in our power. In Mexico City the Government there would be only too pleased to shoot him on sight, but here it is different.

"If he is in England on some legitimate purpose we cannot very well interfere with him. We shall only be able to do so if he is up to some mischief.

"If he is —then, from the brief glimpse I had of him, I should say that he is quite capable of keeping his secrets to himself. However, we may be able to discover a chink in his armour. To see if that is possible I shall send out word to all my London agents this afternoon, and by evening I ought to be able to have a line of some sort on his activities —that is, if he is mixed up in anything shady.

"As for you, senor, you will only spoil everything by assaulting him in public. If I am to help you, it must be along my own lines, and you must do as I suggest. Therefore, I want you to return to your lodgings and remain there quietly. Just as soon as I get to know anything I shall communicate with you at once. Do you understand?"

The cool command in Blake's tones did more than anything else to calm the little Mexican. He agreed without further demur to what Blake suggested, and, with a faithful promise not to make any more public attacks upon Morales, he took himself off to Bloomsbury, where his modest lodgings were situated.

Blake, Tinker, and Gordon Lindsay remained at the table for about half an hour longer. Then they rose, and, while Lindsay went off to the City to attend to his special business, Tinker and Blake returned to Baker Street.

Blake instructed Tinker to get into immediate touch with all his numerous private agents in London —no small matter in itself, considering the number to be telephoned to and given Blake's code instructions.

In the meantime, Blake seated himself at his desk to attend to routine work. He was thus engaged some half an hour later, and Tinker, who had finished his telephoning, was seated at his own desk, when Mrs. Bardell entered to announce that a gentleman was at the door, at the same time holding out a tray on which she had placed a card.

Blake took up the card and read the name. Then his brows lifted a little as he remarked sotto voce to Tinker:

"We seem fated to-day to become mixed up with the Spanish-American race, my lad. From the name and address on this card it appears that another Mexican gentleman wishes to consult me."

"Let 'em all come, guv'nor!" responded Tinker, with a grin. "It has been a pretty dud show up to now, but before we finish we might get some fun out of it!"

Blake smiled.

His idea of fun did not exactly coincide with what Tinker meant by the same word. He nodded to Mrs. Bardell as a sign that the visitor was to be admitted, and sat idly tapping the edge of the desk until the door opened a second time, and a swarthy-looking personage of small stature, and rather elegantly dressed, entered.

He bowed rather elaborately first to Blake, then to Tinker. He gave a second bow when Blake asked him to sit down. Then, when the door had closed after Mrs. Bardell, he gave a glance in Tinker's direction, and said:

"I have come to consult you upon a matter of considerable privacy, Mr. Blake. Would it be possible for the young man to leave?"

"It would not, sir," answered Blake curtly. "The young man is my personal assistant and has my complete confidence. He is fully cognisant of all my affairs."

"Ah! I beg your pardon! I was not aware of that. With your permission, then, I shall explain my business."

"Please do so."

"You are, of course, aware, Mr. Blake, that at the present time full diplomatic relations between Mexico and England are in temporary abeyance, owing to the fact that up to now your Government has not recognised the de facto Government of Mexico?"

"Yes, I am quite aware of that."

"At the same time, my Government finds it absolutely essential to keep representation here, owing to the numerous diplomatic and financial relations that are continually coming up for settlement. I have the honour to be the chief representative, and, of course, we hope very strongly that we shall soon receive recognition by the British Government, as all loyal Mexicans believe that President Obregon is the only man to establish a really stable Government in my country."

As his visitor paused for a moment, Blake gave a non-committal nod. He had no intention of making a statement of his political views —although, privately, he rather inclined to agree with what the other had just said.

"One of the chief difficulties which the Obregon Government has had to fight against is the banditry in the Northern States of Mexico. In fact, some of those States have been in a complete condition of turmoil for several years now, and it is an extremely difficult matter to clean out the rebels, owing to the difficult nature of the country and the ease with which they can continue a guerilla form of warfare against the Government troops. However, slowly but surely we are making headway, and we have hopes that soon we shall have peace there.

"If you know anything about those conditions you will surely have heard of several of the bandit leaders. The notorious Villa, who harassed Chihuahua for five years, has, I am thankful to say, retired to his estates, and takes no further part in the uprisings.

"But his place has been taken by one who is equally dangerous to the Central Government, and a man against whom all our expeditions have ended in failure. I speak of one Pancho Morales."

"I have heard of the gentleman," remarked Blake. "In fact, I believe I saw him no later than this morning."

"Ah! Then you know he is in London! So much the better, sir, for you will more readily understand what I have to say. He has been here for some days, and it is the first time he has ventured out of the security of his hills since he took up arms against the Government. And thus, too, it is the first real chance we have had to lay him by the heels. If we could succeed in doing that we should soon be able to reduce the north to submission. But, naturally, he is out of our reach here in London, and, under the present state of relations existing between your Government and ours, we cannot ask their assistance. Nor have we any means of seeking police aid.

"Nevertheless, I have received a strongly-worded despatch from the Mexican Government instructing me to use every legitimate effort to prevent his return to Mexico. And in that despatch were details of the business which brought him to Europe. It was those details, sir, that inspired me to think of you."

"And they are?"

"I have every reason to believe, Mr. Blake, that Pancho Morales is in England at present for the purpose of secretly purchasing a supply of arms and ammunition which he intends to smuggle into Chihuahua for the purpose of creating an uprising on a larger scale than any before. It is that plot which my Government wishes me to smash, if I may use an English phrase."

"But, senor, even if full recognition has not been given to your Government, the British authorities would not permit a freebooter, such as Morales is, to purchase arms here."

"True, sir. They have informed me to that effect But the difficulty is that I have no definite evidence against Morales, and until I have they can do nothing. That is why I have come to you. When you have read the documents, which I am ready to submit, I am quite sure you will agree that Morales intends to run arms into Mexico if he can.

"And, while your Government would not give its sanction to such a thing, there are more ways than one of purchasing guns and ammunition secretly, as I myself can show you, for in the days of Huerta I did it myself."

Blake smiled grimly. "I quite accept that statement, senor," he said, in reminiscent tones. "I have some knowledge, too, of gun-running. But if Morales is up to this sort of game, why can't you put someone on his trail? You say he has been here for some days. Do you mean to say you haven't had his movements reported?"

"I have had three private agents following him, sir. But he is as cunning as a fox, or else my agents are as stupid as a burro, for he has regularly given them the slip."

"Did you know that he has given out that he was leaving London to-morrow?" asked Blake casually.

The other showed an amazed countenance. "Why, how did you know that, Mr. Blake? It is true, as you say, but I cannot fathom how it came to your knowledge, unless you have personal acquaintance with Pancho Morales."

"Not exactly. Do you know Senor Barbosa, senor?"

"Yes. He has been to see me on several occasions. He was once a wealthy hacienda owner in Chihuahua, but Morales ruined him. You know him then?"

"A little, yes. But to return to your statements, senor. I may say now, that, for certain private reasons, I am not disinclined to do what I can to help you to lay Morales by the heels. As long as that assistance could be given here in England I am ready to agree to do so. But only on the condition that, whether I succeed or fail in getting the evidence you need, you will not ask me to follow it up by going to Mexico. My affairs here would not permit me to do so."

"Why, Mr. Blake, I am perfectly ready to agree to that. If you can utilise your organisation to secure the evidence we need, I shall be extremely grateful, and once I can get something really definite to work on I shall know what to do. If I can but discover if Morales is intending to run a cargo of arms into Mexico, then we shall have a chance of picking him up off the coast there."

"In that case, I shall do what I can, senor. I am not prepared to go into details, but I may say that I have already started in motion certain machinery which would soon give us some sort of a line on what Morales is doing, and I have hopes of discovering something before he leaves London tomorrow —if, indeed, he really intends to do so. If you will send me the documents of which you spoke, I shall go through them in case they may contain some suggestions of value,"

"I have brought them with me, Mr. Blake."

With that the Mexican took out a packet of papers from an inner pocket and handed it across to Blake. Then he rose.

"I have pencilled my private address on the back of my card, sir. I take it you will communicate with me as soon as you have anything to report."

"Quite so, senor. Rest assured I shall lose no time, once I have struck something definite."

After a few more polite words the Mexican took his departure. As soon as he was gone Tinker jumped up and picked up the card the visitor had left on Blake's desk. "Senor Jose Gispert," he read aloud. "Is he of any importance in Mexico, guv'nor?"

"If I recollect rightly, my lad, the gentleman you have just seen is one of Obregon's most trusted agents. I was rather favourably impressed with him."

"He didn't seem a bad sort of prune," rejoined Tinker. "Anyway, you see, guv'nor, it turned out as I said. This bird, Morales, must be a peach. He seems to have them all on the run."

"It is a somewhat curious coincidence that from two entirely different directions should come an appeal to sit in at the game he is playing," confessed Blake. "If it is true, as Senor Gispert suggests, that Morales is secretly buying arms, then it is just possible that we may be able to catch him napping before he gets out of England.

"If we could do so, then we should stand a chance of getting satisfaction for Senor Barbosa, which would please me much more than removing a rebel of the Mexican Government. I feel very sorry for Barbosa, and would like to help him."

"Well, guv'nor, some of our agents ought to be able to get some sort of a line on him. With the full crowd on the qui vive, we have about every possible phase covered."

"Quite true, my lad. It is on that we shall have to depend, I think. Morales can't have been carrying on negotiations of any sort for several days without leaving traces. At any rate, one of us must remain here at Baker Street to receive any reports that come in. As I have some business to attend to in the City, you must be the one to stay.

"I shall go along now, and will probably be back here about tea-time. If anything docs turn up, you will know what to do, and if you think it wise to follow up any clue it will be better for you to leave an explanatory note on my desk before you go."

"Very good, guv'nor!"

A few minutes later Blake took his departure in the Grey Panther, and Tinker settled down at his desk, working in a desultory manner while he waited to see if the machinery he had started in motion would bring any results.

At that moment neither he nor Blake dreamed that a good deal was fated to happen before they were to see each other again.

With an angry exclamation the wireless operator doubled his fists and lunged out at Tinker with all his might. Like lightning Tinker dodged, and retaliated with a wicked upper-cut. Then they went at it hammer and tongs.
(*Chapter 3.*)

IT had just turned four o'clock when the telephone bell rang. Tinker jumped up at once, and when he had taken down the receiver he heard a single word come over the wire that gave him the code name of the person who was calling. The name Tinker recognised at once as a certain shady broker in the East-End of London whom Blake had used for many years as one of his confidential agents. Tinker confirmed the code name by giving a certain number, by which all the secret agents identified Baker Street, when the voice said:

"I have certain information about the party in whom you are interested. Your suspicions concerning him are quite correct. He has made large purchases in this country, which are to be shipped from the port of Cardiff to a destination which I have been unable to discover so far. But the name of the ship by which they will be shipped is the Belle of 'Frisco, a tramp of some fifteen hundred tons.

"Further, the material purchased will appear on the manifest under two classes, one being plantation implements, and the other as whisky. That is all I have been able to discover so far, except the name of the man who is acting in the matter in Cardiff, and also that the party in whom you are interested is expected to arrive in Cardiff to-morrow."

"Good work!" said Tinker, when the voice came to a pause. "That is almost more than we had hoped for. What is the name of the agent in Cardiff?"

"A Chinaman, name of Sam Loo."

"Ho, ho! Sam Loo, eh! I know that Celestial gentleman all right. The Belle of 'Frisco must be one of the ships he usually operates by."

"I don't know about that. Do you wish me to try to get any more information?"

"You might follow up your inquiries, and, if you come on anything of further interest, communicate it here. I shall make note of what you have told me. Your payment slip will come along in due course."

"Thank you! I shall keep up the inquiries, then."

With that the speaker hung up the receiver. Tinker did likewise; then he began walking up and down the room in some excitement.

"This begins to look interesting," he muttered gleefully. "The old chap from the Mexican agency had Morales lined out all right, and it didn't take our system long to get track of what was going on."

Then Tinker grinned. "I shouldn't be in the slightest surprised if our agent, who just telephoned the information, had had considerable to do with that deal in 'plantation implements' and 'whisky' himself. He seemed to be in possession of a lot of details about it.

"Well, that needn't worry us. That is the beauty of the guv'nor's system. 'Set a crook to catch a crook' is a good maxim, and the bunch of crooks who pass along the information to us know just how valuable to them it is to keep in the guv'nor's good graces."

Which was true enough; and it is safe to say that Blake's friend at Scotland Yard, Inspector Thomas, would have been appalled if he had guessed for a single moment how closely associated with the underworld was a part of Sexton Blake's system.

"Sam Loo —Cardiff —the Belle of 'Frisco!" muttered Tinker. "I know that old devil Sam Loo all right. He would be just the right person for Morales to get in touch with, if he wanted to get a contraband shipment of arms out of the country. And Sam Loo has used the Belle of 'Frisco more than a few times in running secret shipments of Chinese into the United States; the Belle and the schooner Eastern Queen used to be the pair working for him at the time he was acting under Prince Wu Ling.

"That is certainly a bit of information of value, and I'll bet the guv'nor will be pleased when he knows it. As for the cargo, 'plantation implements' probably means 'rifles,' and I fancy, if one could see inside the cases of whisky, he would find they were stuffed with ammunition. Not a bad dodge; but the question is, at what point will Morales try and run them into the country?

"Now, Senor Gispert said that if they could keep track of the contraband they would attack Morales as soon as his craft got inside the three-mile limit of Mexican waters. But will Morales risk that? I'm willing to bet he is capable of thinking of another way. If he did, what would he choose?"

Tinker scratched his head and pondered deeply. Almost unconsciously he paused before a large map of the world which hung on the wall over one of the bookcases. He studied it for some time, devoting his scrutiny principally to the sweep of coast-line which made the curve of the Gulf of Mexico.

It was in the lower part of this that the seaboard of the United

States and Mexico met, and it was just at that point, near the mouth of the Rio Grande, that Tinker appeared to find the most interest.

"Now, what would I do if I wanted to run a bunch of arms into Mexico?" he soliloquised aloud. "The guv'nor says if you want to figure out what the other follow is going to do, try and put yourself in his place. Well, let's take this bird. Morales.

"He is a tough customer, all right. More than that, he appears to be the big noise in most of the northern part of Mexico. That means he is practically master of all the country along the Mexican side of the Rio Grande. When he is there he is pretty safe, but, on the other hand, he hasn't any control over the coast; and if he tried to slip through the three-mile limit a Mex gunboat would have a pretty fair chance of nailing him.

"He would certainly figure on that, and try to eliminate that risk. Well, there is one thing certain, that, since the passing of the Eighteenth Amendment in the United States, there has been an enormous system of rum running built up, and, from all accounts, that system has been extended to include undesirable aliens, who otherwise wouldn't have a chance of getting into the United States. That's what the guv'nor says, and he knows what he is talking about.

"Now, Morales would know that too. In fact, I'll bet that he is mixed up in rum running across the Mexican border, and would be hand in glove with the smugglers on the American side. All right, then! Suppose I was Pancho Morales, with a cargo of arms and ammunition that I wanted to get into Mexico, and I knew it would be jolly unhealthy for me to poke my nose inside the Mexican three-mile limit, what would I do?

"I'll bet I'd try to work my contraband in through the United States, and down to the Mexican border, where my own forces were in command of the situation. Scott! I wonder if I have hit on it?"

Tinker drew closer to the map, and, reaching out his hand, placed a finger on the coast of the State of Texas, just near the city of Galveston.

"He might do it somewhere near here," he muttered. "It would be too risky off New Orleans; but then, again, he might try it somewhere off the Florida coast. If he lay outside the three-mile limit, and the rum runners came out to him, he could get his contraband ashore that way. Then they could push it along to the border for him, and his own men could easily transport it across the Rio Grande.

"Perhaps that isn't the way Pancho Morales will try and work it, but, by thunder, if I was going to tackle it, that is the way I would do it. Anyway, the first thing to do is to get a definite line on the Belle of 'Frisco and her cargo. And why the dickens shouldn't I just make tracks for Cardiff this very afternoon? There is no telling what time the guv'nor may turn up, and if Morales is lighting out to-morrow, time is precious. Otherwise, I don't see much chance of nailing him before he slips out of England."

Tinker stood figuring the matter over for some minutes. Then he came to a decision. Seating himself at his desk, he scribbled a hasty note to Blake, informing him what the East-End broker had told him, and adding that he thought it best that he should go off to Cardiff as soon as possible. He wound up by saying that he would communicate at the earliest opportunity after his arrival there.

He sealed the note and laid it on Blake's desk, after which he ran along to his room to pack a bag. Ten minutes later, after telling Mrs. Bardell that he was off, he stepped into the street and walked along until he caught sight of a taxi. He had already looked up the trains, and found that, if he lost no time, he would just make one for Cardiff, and, as a matter of fact, he made it with about two minutes to spare.

What with daylight saving and the long summer twilight, it still lacked a little time before dusk should set in when Tinker arrived at Cardiff and drove through to his hotel. Back in London, Sexton Blake had read his note some three hours before, and, on reaching the hotel, Tinker found a telegram from Blake, which read as follows:

"Your action was correct. Have ascertained, since your departure, that party concerned may motor through Cardiff this evening, and that ship may clear to-morrow morning. Use every effort secure something to-night. Am holding myself in readiness to come on to Cardiff if necessary."

Tinker gave a grunt of satisfaction as he finished reading the message, which be then carefully tore into small pieces.

"That's one time, anyway, I did the right thing," he muttered, with a grin. "But just as like as not the guv'nor would have given me beans for slipping off on my own like this. So our flashy Mex friend may motor to Cardiff this evening, eh! And the Belle of 'Frisco may clear to-morrow morning! I wonder how the guv'nor discovered that?

Probably our crook broker passed it in to him." (Which, in fact, was the correct deduction.)

"Well, anyway, there is a little daylight left. I'll just take a little stroll down to the docks and have a squint at the Belle. If she is going to clear tomorrow morning, there will be signs of it. And if Morales shows up to-night, I guess I'll be on hand."

Tinker lost no time in starting out. Although he hadn't been in Cardiff for some little time, he knew the place well, and had no difficulty in finding his way down to the dingy dock district, where it was not long before he spotted the Belle of 'Frisco.

The moment his eyes lit on the ancient craft he knew it was the same he had seen years ago on the occasion when he and Blake had been out to uncover the underground route by which Sam Loo was slipping Chinese into America.

It had been his first idea to take a squint at the Belle, then to go along to Sam Loo's saloon and see if he could pick up any useful information there. But as he stood gazing at the dingy craft he saw something which caused him to defer his visit to the Chinaman's joint. That something was the aerial of the ship's wireless.

"Hallo!" he muttered, as he examined it from a little distance. "So the old Belle is getting porky in her old days, is she? Fancy that! She must be thirty years old if she is a day, and now they have fitted her with wireless. Must be fairly recently, too, for she didn't have it the last time I saw her. Old Sam Loo must find it necessary in his business to keep up-to-date. I —hallo! Just look who's here! Well, well, well! What next will I see! If that isn't a nice natty young wireless officer just coming ashore from the Belle, I'll eat my hat. We are certainly getting swanky."

He watched the young fellow in peaked cap and brass-buttoned coat, who had just come ashore, as he walked briskly up the dock towards where Tinker stood. He was a lad about Tinker's age and of somewhat the same sturdy build.

But it was obvious that if this wasn't his first wireless billet afloat it was nearly so, for, despite his slight swagger, it was apparent to Tinker that the other was a little self-conscious of his uniform. Tinker was just beginning to grin in enjoyment when suddenly, as if a bolt had struck him from the purpling sky, an idea flashed into his keen young mind.

He did not pause to examine it. Instead, as it broke upon him, he started forward on a course that must bring him across the other's bows, so to say. As they met, Tinker smiled pleasantly.

"Good-evening," he said. "Am I right in thinking you are the wireless operator on the Belle of 'Frisco?"

The other came to a halt and regarded Tinker closely. But when he saw that the lad was no dock loafer, he condescended to reply.

"I am," he answered abruptly.

"I thought so," rejoined Tinker. "And am I also right in supposing that the Belle sails to-morrow?"

"You had better ask the captain that."

"Right! I will."

The other then started on, but Tinker swung round in his tracks, and began to keep pace with him.

"Nice old tub, the Belle," he offered conversationally. "I used to know her years ago. It's extraordinary how she keeps afloat. I guess she's your first one, isn't she?"

"Well, what if she is?" grunted the other lad. "What has that to do with you? And why are you questioning me? I have already told you, if you want to know anything about the ship, go to the captain."

"Keep your shirt on, laddie," advised Tinker, still speaking pleasantly. "I hold a wireless certificate myself. Let's say it was just professional interest, brotherly concern —anything you wish."

The other's tone altered a little.

"I didn't know you were an operator," he said. "But if you are looking for the billet on the Belle of 'Frisco, you won't got it. I have just got it, and I sail to-morrow."

"I don't think so, mate," rejoined Tinker coolly.

The other came to a halt.

"What do you mean?" he asked aggressively.

"Just what I say," rejoined Tinker. "You say you sail on the Belle tomorrow. Sorry to disappoint you, old bean, but you do nothing of the sort. You stay at home, and I sail on the Belle. Do you get me, old son?"

The other's countenance showed indecision. It was plain that he didn't know just what Tinker was driving at —whether the strange lad was pulling his leg, or whether he was another wireless operator who had been after the job, and was determined to get it even then, if he could. He came to the conclusion that the latter was the case.

"You want to turn over and wake up before you have any more

dreams," he snarled. "And another thing; take yourself off. I didn't ask for your company, and I don't like the cut of your jib. I guess you can understand that, can't you?"

Tinker drew up.

"I can —quite!" he said cheerfully. "But I guess we had better understand each other, young feller-me-lad. It's plain to be seen that the good old Belle provides her wireless men with shop-made uniforms, and that one doesn't fit you. Too broad across the chest, laddie, and a little too flappy about the legs. It would suit me much better, and inside the next few minutes there is going to be a swap between you and me. You are going straight back home, laddie, and the captain of the Belle of 'Frisco is going to have a different operator to sail with him. Now, do you get me straight?"

"Oh, go to the dickens!"

With that the other made to walk on, but Tinker shot out his hand and gripped his arm.

"Not so fast," he snapped, his voice now curt and hard. "You heard what I said. We couldn't find a better place for a change than right here behind these coal sheds. Now, get that uniform off, or I will take it off you by force."

The answer came swift and sudden.

With an exclamation of anger, the other young fellow doubled up his fist, and drove it with all his weight, finding, however, nothing but air where Tinker's chin had been the fraction of a second before. Like lightning, Tinker had dodged, and now, as the other sought to recover his balance, Tinker assisted him with a wicked uppercut to the jaw.

Then they were at it hammer and tongs.

Tinker was as ripe as autumn fruit for a mix-up, and he was not the least bit disappointed when he found the other lad as willing as himself to give and take. In physique they were pretty evenly matched, with the difference that Tinker had a little the better of it in the shoulders, while the other had a slight advantage in reach.

But one balanced the other, for it was no case of three-minute rounds with a referee hopping about. It was, each knew, a fight to a finish, and Tinker's opponent knew as well as did he that the winner of that fight was the one who would sail as wireless operator on the Belle of 'Frisco.

TINKER took things cautiously for the first few minutes, until he had pretty well gauged the other's method of fighting. He soon discovered that he himself held a good deal of advantage in experience, but the other had a natural crouch that was extremely difficult to get past. His footwork, too, was good, and the two combined gave him a natural defence that would have made him no mediocre fighter if he had been handled properly. He had some weakness in his attack, however, and it was on that that Tinker concentrated.

He gave him no rest from the very start of the mill. He kept hammering away at the defence until, by sheer weight, he got his man on the move. Tinker was watching like a cat for the slightest opening, and when it came he was in under the guard like lightning.

Then he bored in, and for the next few minutes there was as pretty a bit of in-fighting as one could wish to see. Time and again Tinker avoided a clinch. He was watching for a chance to bring up a jolt to the "button," and he was determined, if he got home with it a second time, it would do its work.

The other sensed this, as he also sensed Tinker's superiority in a close mix-up, and he accordingly kept his chin covered at the expense of yielding his body to Tinker's terrific battering.

But such a pace could not last for long. Something had to break.

Either Tinker's attack must diminish in its power of punishment, or the other's guard must come down to cover up on the "cellar." And it was the latter who yielded first.

As Tinker got home two terrific jabs, his opponent gave a grunt and sagged a little. He could no more have prevented himself from dropping his guard than he could have withstood a pile-driver.

And Tinker wasn't asking for any better chance. Like a young tiger he was there with an upper-cut which caught his man full on the point; then, easing back just a little, Tinker flashed out a beautiful, clean "haymaker" that send his man down as if he had been poleaxed.

Tinker stepped back, panting.

"Some useful little scrap!" he muttered, rubbing his fist against a rising lump above his right eye. "Not a bad laddie with his dukes, either. If he developed that attack of his, he might be a pretty tough handful at that. But I guess it is settled now who sails on the Belle."

With that he dropped to his knees, and took his late antagonist's head on his knee. He glanced round until he saw a water-tap projecting from the wall of a nearby coalshed.

He laid the other's head back, and, grabbing up his cap, which had been knocked off during the mill, ran across to the tap. He turned the water on full until the cap, though leaking freely, was full; then he raced back, and dashed the contents into the upturned face of the prostrate one. He repeated his crude treatment three times, and at last had the satisfaction of seeing the other's eyes open.

He struggled to a sitting posture, and regarded Tinker groggily.

"W-wha' shtru' me?" he mumbled vaguely.

"A nice mild little 'haymaker.' laddie," returned Tinker cheerfully. "Likewise, the new wireless operator of the Belle of 'Frisco."

The last words seemed to reach the slowly-clearing mind of the other; for, after frowning over them for a few seconds, he glanced up again.

"Wha's matter, anyway?" he managed to articulate. "Whash reason you set on me like that?"

Tinker squatted on his heels.

"Now, listen, laddie." he said quietly. "I have nothing against you; and, take it from me, I am jolly sorry I had to knock you out to make you listen to sense. You are a game bird, and that is enough for me. But I have very particular and private reasons why I want to leave England to-morrow by the Belle of 'Frisco. I am no claim-jumper, and I don't want to push you out of your job. But there is no other way. All the same, you won't lose anything by it. I'll see to that."

"How can you?" asked the other bitterly. "If you want to know, that job I landed to-day is my first billet. I need it badly, and it is a dirty trick for you to butt in. You may have beaten me, but you can't take that billet."

"You don't get me straight," responded Tinker patiently. "I have already told you I am no claim-jumper. But I must have that job. Look here, what is your name?"

"Baxter."

"Well, let me tell you something in confidence. That hooker is no good —or, at least, I should say the gang aboard her is no good. You won't do any good for yourself by sailing on her. It will only give you a black eye for your next billet. She is carrying cargo that is going to get her into trouble before her run is finished, and that is why you will be well advised to keep away."

"If that is so, why do you want to sail in her?"

"That is a fair question, and you have a right to an answer. But, first, I want to know if I can trust you not to blab?"

"I'm no nark. If the ship is a wrong 'un, what's that to me? I need the job and the money."

Tinker offered his cigarette-case, and, after the two had got a weed going, he said in a low tone:

"I am going to take you into my confidence to a certain extent, Baxter. I am going to trust you not to blab; but if you do, I promise you I will give you a beating that will make this evening seem like a pink tea in comparison. Now, listen! Ever hear of Sexton Blake, the criminologist?"

"Of course," grunted Baxter scornfully. "What do you think I am —a Hottentot?"

"Well, even at that, there are several Hottentots who have heard of him," rejoined Tinker. "However, if you have heard of him, you have possibly heard of his assistant?"

"You mean Tinker?"

"Just that. Well, young fellow-me-lad, I am Tinker."

The other glanced at him incredulously for a few moments. Young Baxter had had a comparatively uneventful life until fate started to give him a whirl that evening, and, while he had read a good deal of the doings of the famous Sexton Blake and his almost equally famous assistant, he had never contemplated meeting either of them face to face, much less milling it for a quarter of an hour with Tinker. But, though he was inclined to doubt Tinker's statement, something in the lad's tone told him that it was true.

"You may doubt it if you wish," went on Tinker, "but I will show you proof before we finish. It is enough for now that I am Tinker, and that I have very urgent reasons for sailing on the Belle of 'Frisco as wireless operator. Now, here is what I am prepared to do. If you will trade that uniform for my suit, and clear out, I will give you twenty-five pounds in cash as a bonus. That is more than you would get on the voyage on which the Belle is bound, and you would be able to get another job soon. If you can't, I pledge you my word that the guv'nor will see that you get one. If you don't accept those terms, I shall have to take the uniform by force, and in that case you don't get any cash bonus. What about it?"

"Are you honestly Sexton Blake's assistant?"

"On my honour."

"Well, then, I guess there isn't anything else for me to do. I give in."

"Sensible laddie. Now, let's get in behind this shed and change. Then you can come to my hotel with me, and I will give you written proof that I am Tinker. By the way, where is your home?"

"Birmingham."

"Good! In that case you can keep right on travelling. I will fix things with the skipper of the Belle all right. Why had you come ashore this evening?"

"Just to get a few things before we sailed."

"Where is your cabin?"

"Adjoining the wireless-room."

"Had you to report to the captain when you returned?"

"No."

"Good! That means I can go aboard and go straight to the cabin, then I sha'n't have to face the skipper until to-morrow, and, if luck is with me, it may not be until after we have got away."

"The Belle is due to sail at five o'clock. If you are careful you ought to be able to manage that."

"You leave it to me, laddie. Now, off with those duds."

The two effected a rapid exchange, and, in the now deepening dusk, it was difficult to see very much difference between them.

That completed, Tinker gave a sign, and, as if there had never been such a thing as a dispute between them, they went off through the gathering dusk arm in arm towards Tinker's hotel.

There Tinker kept his promise about still further proving his identity, after which he handed the wireless operator the amount he had pledged himself to pay over.

After arranging that he should heave Baxter's trunk on to the dock some time during the night, so that the latter could pick it up before leaving for Birmingham, they shook hands and parted, Tinker to complete a few matters before going on board the Belle of 'Frisco, while the other was to lie low until an opportunity should occur for him to reach the dock unseen and claim his trunk.

Tinker's first duty was to draft a long explanatory telegram to Blake, which he filed for dispatch early the following morning. Then, after paying his hotel bill, he got hold of a porter and handed over his bag to be carried to the dock at which the Belle was moored.

By now darkness had completely enveloped the docks, and only a few wharf and riding-lights broke the gloom. After stumbling about in the region of the coal-sheds for some time, they at last managed to reach the dock which was their objective, and at the bottom of the gangway Tinker dismissed the porter.

Taking the bag, he mounted the gangway, finding as he reached the top that a sailor was lounging there on duty. He gave a cursory glance at Tinker as the latter stepped on to the deck, but in the darkness he apparently took him for the new wireless operator returning from his expedition ashore.

Tinker gave a grunt, which might have meant anything, and, striding along the deck, made for the squat house amidships, which he knew must be the wireless-room and the operator's cabin. The door of the wireless-room was on the hook, so, after easing his bag to the deck, Tinker lifted the hook and entered.

When he had felt for the switch and had turned the light on he found that he had made no mistake. He was in the wireless-room, and a brief scrutiny showed him that the equipment was thoroughly up to date. He had not been very much worried on that account, for Tinker had been a close and enthusiastic student of both wireless telegraphy and wireless telephony for several years, and was a thoroughly competent operator of every type of installation.

In fact, he had made one or two minor, but none the less ingenious, inventions himself, and had spoken only the truth when he had informed Baxter that he was fully certificated as an operator.

He dragged the bag in after him and closed the door. Then he sat down before the table on which the sending key had been fixed, and devoted ten minutes or so to a more detailed examination of the installation.

Now, even at that moment, Tinker had formed no really definite line of action for the immediate future. His chief aim had been to get on board the Belle in some sort of recognised position which would enable him to try and discover if the old hooker was really about to put to sea with contraband arms and ammunition for the Mexican rebels. The sudden appearance of the regular operator had given him his inspiration, and that, followed by physical supremacy, had placed him in the position he had sought.

But he realised only too well that this was but a first step in the game he had to play that night.

He had no intention or desire to go to sea on the Belle of 'Frisco unless it became absolutely imperative. If Blake's information was correct, then whatever he did would have to be done that very night. It was now getting on for eleven o'clock, and, if the Belle sailed the following morning, it meant he would have, roughly speaking, about six hours in which to work.

On the other hand, if there should be a flaw in the information passed on to Blake —if Pancho Morales should not come through to Cardiff that evening, but should defer his departure from London until the morrow as he himself had announced at the Venetia, then it would give Tinker anything up to twenty-four hours in which to work.

And he reckoned that would be quite sufficient for his purpose. But if Morales should turn up, and if the Belle should slip out early in the morning, then it was not going to be so easy.

So far he had noticed but a single man on watch. But if this was the last evening in port it was very likely that most of the crew had been given shore leave, which meant that they were apt to come straggling aboard any time during the next hour or so. What officers were still aboard he couldn't tell, nor did he hanker to find out just then. It was his game to keep clear of the captain for the present.

The discovery that the wireless operator who was now in possession of the wireless-room was not the one originally engaged might cause some inconvenient questions. If the Belle was being used for contraband purposes, both officers and crew would be inclined to be suspicious of anything out of the normal.

Tinker knew that the only way for him to find out if the contraband was actually on board was to make an investigation of the contents of the hold.

If he came upon anything resembling the cases which Blake's agent had said were stated on the manifest to be "plantation implements," and the other cases which were put down as "whisky," then he would know that he was on a warm scent. Once he could ascertain that, he could find an opportunity of slipping ashore and taking measures there to have the Belle of 'Frisco detained until a more thorough examination could be made.

On the other hand, without anything definite he would only have himself laughed at for his pains.

But how to get into the hold?

That was the question which he found decidedly knotty to answer. Even with only one man on watch, he could hardly go out on deck and force off one of the hatch covers. Apart from the noise he would make, he might be discovered at any moment by one of the officers aft, or by some of the crew returning from shore leave. And yet, that seemed the only way if he were to discover the truth.

He hadn't much doubt that he could deal with the solitary watchman. If necessary, he could manage to attack him unawares and put him hors de combat until he had achieved his purpose.

If he could only be sure that his investigation of the hold would yield the something definite he needed, he would not have hesitated to put this idea into effect. But if he should fail —if he should find it necessary to remain on the Belle then, when the showdown came, as it must soon after sailing, the discovery that he was not the man who had been engaged for the job might cause him to be suspected of such an attack on the watchman.

It seemed a problem utterly impossible of solution. And yet, he was determined to solve it before the hour of midnight struck. What to do? What could he do?

Seated before the instrument table he was revolving the pros and cons over and over in his mind, and had come to no decision when, suddenly, his attention was attracted by the sound of voices outside. Rising, he crossed the wireless-room and switched off the lights.

Then he opened the door and peered out. Just outside the door was a bulky supporting stanchion, and, like a shadow, Tinker glided out and took cover behind this.

Screwing his head round, he was in time to see a lantern moving about near the head of the gangway, and in the circle of light it cast he could make out three figures standing in a little group.

Just then they moved aside as by one accord, and Tinker made out a blurred shape which came up over the side. A second later he was able to identify this as a trunk being carried by two men. They came aboard, and, in obedience to a curt command, made aft with the trunk.

Then the other figures followed, and, as the bearer of the lantern turned, the light fell for the space of a moment on the features of the taller of the trio. As he glimpsed them Tinker shrank back.

"Morales," he breathed. "So the guv'nor's tip was correct! That means the Belle will clear in the morning as Baxter said. Good night to any chance I will have to-night of getting a peep at what is in the hold. It will need all the finesse I can bring to get Baxter's trunk over the side. In fact, I am afraid that young man will have to say good-bye to it. If I raise suspicions now, I'm done for."

He slipped back into the wireless-room, closed the door and switched on the light again. Then he crossed to a door facing him. He opened it, and, from the light which shone through from behind him, he saw that it was a small, but not uncomfortable cabin.

Tinker entered and sat down on Baxter's cabin trunk, which still stood close to the bunk just as the other had left it. He sat for some time in deep thought. Finally, he gave a grunt.

"Nothing for it but that," he muttered. "I won't have a ghost of a chance to-night, therefore the only thing to do is to sail with the ship. And Baxter's trunk must come, too. I daren't take the risk. But one thing is lucky —as wireless operator, I ought to be able to keep in touch with the guv'nor, part of the time at least.

"And I guess the next move is his."

"THE reckless young ass."

As Sexton Blake uttered the words he pushed back his chair from the breakfast table and made his way into the consulting-room. In one hand he carried several letters and telegrams which Mrs. Bardell had laid beside his place, and it was after reading two of the latter messages that Blake had given vent to his annoyance.

"The reckless young ass!" he reiterated, as he sat down at his desk. "Now, what the dickens did he want to take a step like that for without finding out whether I should approve or disapprove? Why couldn't he have stuck to his original intention?"

With this he spread out the two messages which had been the cause of his perturbation, and read them again. The first one, which did not cause his expression to alter, was the one Tinker had sent from the hotel in Cardiff the night before, in which he advised Blake that he had secured means of getting aboard the Belle of 'Frisco, and that he hoped during the night to discover something definite regarding the contraband which the Belle was suspected of having in her holds.

With all that Blake entirely agreed.

But it was the second —a wireless message sent from the Belle, after she had put to sea, that had caused him to frown at the breakfast table, and now caused that same frown to deepen.

It ran as follows:

"Am aboard as wireless operator; put to sea this morning at five; off Lundy Island now; our man aboard, but was impossible last night discover anything definite; thought best come along as can keep in touch frequently through wireless; am relaying this through Cornwall, and will receive any messages you send providing they come along between twelve noon and eight evening or between twelve midnight and eight morning; other hours apprentice is on duty listening-in; nothing definite report so far but expect have interview with captain this morning owing method of securing post —anticipate some trouble, but think will dispose all right; try tell me what you propose doing and what you wish me to do if discover material actually on board —T."

That was the message which had upset Blake's equilibrium, and it is little wonder that it had done so. He had sent Tinker off to Cardiff to make certain inquiries there, but it had been no part of his intention that the lad should go to such lengths as it seemed he had gone, if the wireless message was genuine, and from its phrasing Blake felt it was.

If Tinker had failed to discover anything incriminating while the Belle of 'Frisco was in port, it had been Blake's plan to put certain machinery into motion before the ship sailed. If that failed to produce results, then it had been his intention to abandon the case, for the present at least. He had already made it quite clear that it would be most inconvenient for him to cross the Atlantic at that time, and he meant it.

But now, with Tinker already at sea, the whole business had become considerably complicated. It was difficult to tell just what steps he should take. If there was no contraband on the Belle, then Tinker was on a wild goose chase; and it would mean just so much time wasted.

On the other hand, if the contraband arms were there, then, in dealing with a man like Pancho Morales, and the captain of the Belle (for Blake knew that pirate of old), then Tinker might conceivably run into a hornets' nest of the worst description. It would assist him considerably in deciding what to do, Blake thought, if he only knew what exactly the conditions were under which Tinker had gained his position on the ship.

All that Blake knew, so far, was that, in some way, the lad had managed to get there as wireless operator, but under what circumstances, it was not exactly clear. All he could deduce was that the lad had used some form of finesse, and, that being so, then his situation might be a decidedly delicate one.

He was still frowning over this thought when there came a tap at the door, and Mrs. Bardell entered. She announced that a young man was asking to see Blake, and, after an absent-minded glance at the clock, Blake nodded his head. A few seconds later he glanced up to see a sturdy young fellow enter the consulting-room. Blake's eyes noted swiftly that he was wearing a cap and suit exactly similar to those which Tinker had worn the previous day, and, like a flash, his keen mind jumped the gap to the identity of the young fellow before him.

"You are, or were, the wireless operator on the Belle of 'Frisco," he said, before the lad had a chance to speak. "You must have come through from Cardiff on the early-morning train. Have you a message for me from my assistant."

The lad was standing gazing at Blake in open-mouthed amazement. He had begun to have doubts of Tinker after all, when, after hanging about the dock half the night, he had seen the Belle pull out without his trunk being set on the dock. He had decided therefore to go to London to see Sexton Blake, instead of going on to his home in Birmingham, as he had originally intended. Hence his early appearance at Baker Street.

But while he had read a great deal, and heard a great deal, of the famous criminologist, Sexton Blake, and his extraordinary powers of analysis and deduction, he had never come face to face with the great man. Hence Blake's rapid, but, in reality, very simple, deduction left him gaping.

"Y-yes, sir," he stuttered inanely, "I am the wireless operator from the Belle of 'Frisco, b-but h-how did you know, sir?"

Blake smiled.

"Sit down, my lad," he said. "How did I know? Very simple. You are wearing the suit and cap which my assistant, Tinker, was wearing yesterday. It is a little on the loose side for you, which leads me to conclude that it wasn't originally made for you. Moreover, I have just received a wireless message from my assistant informing me that he is on the Belle as wireless operator; therefore the connection was not difficult. But I am a little curious to know just how he managed to persuade you to allow him to take your place. Er —am I correct in concluding that the lump over your left eye, and that partially-closed right eye, have anything to do with it?"

Baxter grinned a little sheepishly.

"Yes, sir, you are correct," he said. "I will tell you just what happened."

Forthwith he began to relate everything that had happened from the moment when Tinker accosted him on the dock, until they had parted at the hotel. Then he went on to tell Blake how he had hung about the docks half the night waiting for the appearance of his trunk, but how he had seen the Belle warp out, taking the box with her.

"I thought then he must be a fake," he said. "So I thought I would come on to London and see you, sir. I thought, if there was a young fellow masquerading as your assistant, you ought to know it. Also, sir, I thought it a good chance to look for another job."

"He was not deceiving you," remarked Blake, after a short pause. "It was my assistant, but I had no idea he intended to sail by the Belle of 'Frisco. Let's see now, my lad, just when did you get the billet?"

"Yesterday morning, sir.

"Were you aboard most of the day?"

"Yes, sir."

"Was she still loading cargo?"

"Some, sir —not a great deal."

"Now, think well, my lad. Did you see any longish cases which might, for example, contain, say, tools for plantation work?"

"Well, sir, there were several cases of that description. I remember because I was standing by the apprentice who was checking them up on the manifest. They were on the manifest, I think, as plantation implements."

"Ah, yes. And did the Belle take any cases of whisky aboard, do you know?"

Baxter grinned.

"I should say she did, sir. A good many cases at that."

"Um. Quite interesting —decidedly interesting, I should say. Do you know her exact destination?"

"No, sir —that is not the port; but the apprentice said something about clearing for Tampico."

"Do you know anything about a special passenger she was to take?"

"No, sir; except that someone was expected from London. But I don't know whether it was one of the owners or not. The Belle is not a passenger vessel."

"No —I know that," rejoined Blake, a little grimly. "Well, my lad, I am glad you decided to come on to London to see me. You have given me one or two bits of information that I wanted. Now then, what about yourself? I think you said that my assistant had given you a bonus of twenty-five pounds?"

"Yes, sir."

"And you want to find another billet?"

"Yes, sir."

"Well, I think I can help you in that. I shall give you a letter to a friend of mine, and I fancy he will see that you get something. Will that do?"

"I shall be most grateful, sir."

Blake swung round in his seat, and, drawing some paper towards him, began to write. In the meantime, his young visitor occupied himself by taking in his surroundings. He could scarcely realise that he was actually in the consulting-room of the famous Sexton Blake, and that, instead of finding a hard-featured person who would growl at him, he had a kindly, grave-faced man of the world. It was a distinct revelation to him.

And by the time he left, with the letter Blake had given him tucked safely into an inner pocket, he was just one more of the crowd of people here and there in the world who looked upon Blake with a feeling closely akin to worship. And yet he felt, as he looked into those steel-grey eyes, that he would rather almost anything than to be one of those whom Blake would set out to hunt.

Which showed that young Baxter had quite a wholesome supply of understanding.

As soon as he was gone Blake whipped out of his chair and took down a file of morning papers which Mrs. Bardell, in Tinker's absence, had arranged neatly in readiness for his perusal. He turned to the shipping announcements and studied one after the other, until his eye came to rest on one about half-way down the second column.

"Um! Bretonic sailing from Liverpool to-morrow morning. Might make it all right if I can get things cleared up here. Darned annoying, but nothing else to do; never tell what that reckless young ass will run into; better take Barbosa along in case anything comes of it. Um, communicate with Senor Gispert, too; have to telegraph Bryant Kennedy to expect me; get a wireless off to Tinker, too; Bretonic ought to be in New York some days before the old Belle of 'Frisco sights the other side; give me a bit of time to arrange matters there. Um, only thing to do."

With that Blake laid down the file and set to work.

His first act was to telephone the shipping offices of the Bretonic in order to book a passage. Then he telephoned to Senor Barbosa, instructing him to come round to Baker Street as soon as possible.

Following that, he communicated to Senor Gispert, at the Mexican agency, his intention of sailing the next day.

After that he drafted a long cable to Bryant Kennedy, his New York correspondent; and, finally, before setting to work to try to clear up the pressing matters which needed his attention before leaving, he sent off a wireless message to Tinker, advising him what he intended doing, and telling him that if he failed to communicate with him while crossing in the Bretonic, Tinker was to get in touch by wireless with Kennedy as soon as the Belle of 'Frisco should get some way across the Atlantic.

He warned Tinker, at the same time, not to take too many risks in trying to wireless him to the big liner.

That done, he set to work, and was going at high pressure when Senor Barbosa arrived. Briefly Blake explained what was afoot, and then sent the old man off to his lodgings to pack up and be ready to join him late that evening, when he should leave for Liverpool.

One break he made in the afternoon in order to dash off to the bank in the Grey Panther in order to get the necessary funds for the journey. Then he was back at work again, and not until it was time to snatch a hasty snack just before leaving for the station did he desist.

And just before starting out he received a second wireless message from Tinker, which contained the single laconic word.

"Right."

Thus it was that while the ancient Belle of 'Frisco lumbered round the south of Ireland, the leviathan Bretonic was racing down the Irish Sea on one of her record-breaking dashes from Liverpool to New York.

And, leaning on the rail, with a keen gaze sweeping the sea in case they should pass near to the old Belle, was Sexton Blake, while beside him, smiling with renewed hope, was the little Mexican whom Pancho Morales had ruined in every way that a man can be ruined.

"THERE is something deucedly queer about this, Kennedy. I can't quite get the hang of it. Either Tinker has made a mistake, or —"

"Well, it's there plain enough, Blake, and the operator is positive he made no mistake in taking it down."

"I know that; but, nevertheless, things don't look right. For instance, every day, for the past three days, Tinker has given us the position of the Belle of 'Frisco. Right! Now then, his position yesterday was, roughly, not counting the minutes and seconds, 25 degrees north latitude, 78 degrees west longitude.

"Well, here in this message we have an S.O.S. call from the Belle of 'Frisco, saying her position is, roughly, 26 degrees north latitude, 94 degrees west longitude. Just look at that —a difference of sixteen degrees since yesterday in the position of longitude, with only one degree difference in latitude; but that one degree shows her farther to the north than yesterday.

"I tell you, Kennedy, it doesn't seem reasonable to me. I know that old hooker too well to believe for a single moment that she could make all that westerly gain in twenty-four hours.

"Moreover, from what Tinker has been able to tell us, we can feel pretty certain that she is heading across the Gulf of Mexico, not into Mexican waters, or for Tampico, as the captain would have it believed; but, in my opinion, for some rendezvous off the American coast, but as close to the Mexican line as he dare risk it."

"He might be making for a point off Brownsville," ventured Kennedy.

"He might at that, or some point not far distant. Anyway, I am willing to gamble that he will keep out of Mexican waters while he has that cargo of contraband on board. But that doesn't explain this discrepancy. And I don't understand the S.O.S. call. It was not a general S.O.S. to any vessel in the vicinity, but a direct call to this Revenue cutter. That is the most incomprehensible part of the whole thing."

Blake paused there and stood gazing frowningly across the dancing white-tipped blue of the gulf, while Kennedy pondered on the words Blake had just uttered. They were standing on the small bridge of the United States Revenue cutter Mobile, in which they had

38

travelled down from Newport News at a clinking rate.

For the moment they were alone on the bridge, with the exception of a young lieutenant, who was standing at the other end scanning the empty horizon ahead.

On arriving at New York Blake had been met by Bryant Kennedy, and, as soon as he had explained the reason for his rush journey, Kennedy had produced a wireless message which he had received from Tinker that same morning.

It had given the position of the Belle of 'Frisco as she had been at the moment of sending, and, after an examination of the chart on the Bretonic, they found the old tub was still wallowing along just a little more than half-way across.

It was evident that the message to Kennedy was the first one Tinker had been able to get through since approaching the American side.

Blake had not attempted to send any messages to the lad from the Bretonic. He considered it unwise, and hardly expected to receive anything from Tinker unless very important developments should take place the Belle. In his wireless to Kennedy, Tinker had added that he had ascertained that the material was on board, and, of course, Blake knew this meant the lad had located the contraband. So far, so good; but their most immediate problem was to decide the next step.

It was then that both Blake and Kennedy did exactly what Tinker had done back in the consulting-room in Baker Street. They had tried to put themselves in Morales' place, and, from that angle, decide how they would act if their aim was a similar one. And the result of this had not been very different from that at which Tinker had also arrived.

They figured and agreed that Morales was not likely to head into Mexican waters with the contraband on board, for he would know only too well that every craft the Mexican Government could muster would be on the watch for him. If they spotted him they would sink him on sight, and ask questions afterwards.

It seemed far more plausible that Morales; realising this, would prefer to take advantage of one of the well-organised rum-running systems which are to be found the whole way along the four borders of the United States —on the sea borders as well as along the land borders

It seemed also reasonable to suppose that, since he controlled such a large area of Northern Mexico, he would be more likely to choose a system as near to the Mexican border as possible, rather than one more distant, which would entail the additional risk of getting his contraband through a larger number of watchful preventive men.

When they had decided that this was the safest line to follow, it had not taken Kennedy long to press a fast Revenue cutter into service. The speedy Mobile had been placed at their disposal, and, together with Senor Barbosa, they had dashed out of Newport News and down past Hatteras at the best clip the Mobile could make.

After passing Hatteras, Blake had risked sending a message to Tinker, in which he gave a brief outline of what they proposed doing, and urging the lad to keep them posted as often as possible of the exact position of the Belle of Frisco from day to day.

For a day and a half no reply had come from Tinker, but then once a day he had managed to wireless through the approximate position of the old hooker. This information was invaluable to them, for by it they were able to set a course which should eventually bring them across the line which the Belle was following.

But about half an hour before Blake had voiced his puzzlement on the bridge, an urgent S.O.S. had come through from the Belle, sent direct to the Mobile, which had read as follows:

"Revenue cutter Mobile, or any station receiving. —Steamer Belle of Frisco in distress, needing assistance. Position: Latitude, 26 deg. 20 min. north; longitude, 94 deg. 40 min. west. Hurry!"

It was that message which had puzzled Blake, and for more reasons than one. Some of these reasons have already been detailed in his conversation with Kennedy. But equally important, in Blake's mind, was the fact that the message had been sent individually to the Mobile before the mention of any land receiving-stations, which might, in the ordinary course of things, be expected to pick it up, not counting any other ships in the vicinity. At last Blake spoke again.

"You see, Kennedy," he said, slowly and thoughtfully, "as far as we know, Tinker is the only person aboard the Belle of 'Frisco who is supposed to know that the Revenue cutter Mobile is anywhere near the Gulf of Mexico. Of course, when we rounded Key West, and struck the gulf, the Government station at Key West very likely picked up our position and gave it out. In that case, it would be picked up by the station at Guatanamo, as well as by other ships.

"But even at that, since Tinker is the only operator on the Belle of

'Frisco, he wouldn't be likely to hand on the information to anyone else. For that reason I am doubly suspicious. You see, if Tinker really sent this message, and was a free agent at the time of sending, then it means that it is quite genuine, and that the Belle is in distress. On the other hand, if Tinker did not send it, or it was sent under duress, then it is a fake; and, since I am firmly convinced that the Belle of 'Frisco could not cover those sixteen degrees since yesterday, I am inclined to the latter view."

"Maybe someone else on the Belle picked up the position of the Mobile, Blake. Tinker couldn't be on duty twenty-four hours a day."

Suddenly Blake hammered on the rail of the bridge.

"Great guns, Kennedy, I believe you have hit it! How infernally stupid of me! In his first wireless to me, Tinker stated than an apprentice would be listening-in at certain periods of the day. That means the apprentice can read Morse, even if he can't send.

"Which makes it entirely possible he may have heard our position given out by Key West, and passed it on to the captain of the Belle in the ordinary course of his report. That puts another complexion on it. The message may have been ticked off by the apprentice unknown to Tinker, or— But no, for it was received by us half an hour ago. It is now three in the afternoon. According to the schedule Tinker gave me, he was to be on day duty from twelve midday until eight at night, so it must have been sent during his spell of duty. And yet —yet, Kennedy, it looks fishy to me!"

"You mean it looks like a trap?"

"That, or — Wait! Here comes the operator, and it looks as if he had another message. Let us see what it is."

They stood waiting while the young wireless officer came up the ladder. He carried a slip of paper, which he handed to Blake, and stood waiting while Blake read it.

Blake's eyes scanned the words swiftly; then he swung sharply to Kennedy.

"Listen!" he said quickly. "I felt there was something wrong. Listen to this: 'Mobile former message fake. Position is —' It finishes there. Is that all you got, Sparks?"

"Yes, sir. It seems a funny message to me, Mr. Blake. Looks as if the sender had been going to give us his position but something prevented him from doing so. I tried again and again to get through, but nothing doing."

"Nor will you," answered Blake grimly. "The rest of this message would have come through unless the sender had been forcibly prevented from completing it. It is enough to tell me that something serious has happened on the Belle of 'Frisco, which means that something has happened to Tinker. We must get hold of Captain Gilson at once. That hooker must be picked up, and we won't find her at the fake position she has wirelessed to-day."

With that Blake swung down the ladder and set off aft to find the commander, while Kennedy scrambled down and followed. He knew from the expression in Blake's eyes that something was going to break soon.

As Tinker entered the saloon he saw that rumour had not lied, for, seated at the end of the table was Jonas Pettigrew. "Well, who are you?" growled the skipper. "I have taken Baxter's place, sir!" answered Tinker civilly. (*Chapter 7.*)

TINKER had made no mistake when he opined that after the arrival of Morales on board he would find it an impossibility to pursue his investigations in the direction of the ship's hold. From that moment the deck, which had been so silent, and guarded by but a single watchman when Tinker came over the side, immediately became a scene of bustle. As if Morales coming had been a signal, the afterguard showed up on deck, and, from the different voices and remarks he was able to catch, Tinker reckoned that in addition to Morales, the captain, at least one officer, and, he thought, an apprentice, must be among the number.

Then, too, the crew began to straggle along in twos and threes, and a little later his ear detected the unmistakable sounds which always attend upon a ship being got ready to warp out.

At that he gave it up. He knew perfectly well that it would jeopardise the success of his whole scheme if he put in an appearance then. In fact, he heard one inquiry as to the whereabouts of "Sparks," and made out someone answering that he had come aboard some time before.

That was apparently all that the questioner wanted to know, for he was not disturbed. As he could do nothing more then, and as he had finally made up his mind to stick by the ship, Tinker, who was a good deal of a philosopher in his way, decided to turn in and get some sleep, in anticipation of more strenuous hours on the morrow.

In five minutes he was in dreamland; nor did he wake again until he felt the rattle of the ancient engines as the Belle got under way. Tinker gave a passing thought to Baxter, wondering what the lad would think when he saw no signs of his trunk. But that had to wait for an explanation later on.

Tinker knew that had he attempted to push the box over the side the previous evening, questions were bound to be asked.

As he looked out the porthole of his cabin he saw that they were already well out in the Channel.

After washing, he got into his uniform and went into the wireless-room, he had left the door on the hook before turning in, and now through the opening he spied a cabin-boy making his way aft with a loaded tray.

Tinker signalled the lad, and curtly bade him bring him some

44

coffee; then he turned his attention to the wireless instrument, which was his only connection with Blake. Also, he kept his back studiously turned towards the door when the cabin boy entered with his coffee and rolls.

"Just as well to be careful!" he thought. "Before I go down to face the old man I want to get a message through to the guv'nor. I fancy I can pick up the Land's End station all right. Then I'll wait until the old man has had his breakfast. Wonder who the skipper is, anyway? Seems to me I heard somewhere that old Jonas Pettigrew, who used to be the skipper on the Eastern Queen, had been transferred to the Belle. If he has, then I shall have to watch out. I guess he won't recognise me in this get-up, but if he did —oh, my, there would be one sudden vacancy in the ranks of wireless operators!"

The cabin-boy, who, as a matter of fact, had only had one fleeting glimpse of Baxter the previous day, evidently saw nothing strange about the young man at the table, for he set down the tray and went out without offering any remark.

Tinker soon demolished the contents of the tray, for he was hungry. After that he seated himself again before the instrument and began to tune up. He had little fear of this rousing suspicion, for it was a perfectly natural thing for an operator to test his installation, and, in doing so, to carry on a conversation with other stations ashore and afloat. His only danger would be if there was anyone aboard who knew the code, and who might be close enough to the wireless-room to overhear the tapping out of the message. One definite danger regarding this was, he knew, the apprentice.

He had been told by Baxter what hours the apprentice would be on duty to relieve him, but he knew enough about ship routine to figure that this arrangement would not come into effect until the evening spell. In this he proved correct.

They were just off Lundy, when, after picking up Land's End station, Tinker tapped out the message which was to be read by Sexton Blake while at breakfast that same morning. Then, with that off his mind, Tinker rose and passed out, determined to beard the skipper without further delay.

As he passed along the waist he glanced up at the bridge, and noted a single figure there. It was certainly not Jonas Pettigrew, and Tinker reckoned the man was too young to be skipper. So he kept on aft, until he came to the companionway leading down to the saloon.

He descended the steps with a firm tread, and as he stepped into the saloon he discovered that wherever he had heard the rumour it was correct, for seated at one end of the long table was none other than Jonas Pettigrew, one time skipper of the Eastern Queen, and now apparently in command of the Belle of 'Frisco.

A couple of places down on his left was an officer whom Tinker reckoned was the engineer. Lower down still was a young fellow whom it was obvious could only be the apprentice, and at the near end of the table, with his back to Tinker, was the bulky figure of Pancho Morales.

The other side of the table had three places set, but at the moment they were unoccupied.

Tinker saluted, and, walking along between the chairs and the sloping side of the saloon, paused beside the skipper's place. The latter had taken scarcely any notice of him at first, but now he glanced up. As he did so, Tinker noticed that the Yankee-cut beard was a little greyer than when he had last seen Pettigrew, and that the hatchet-shaped Yankee features were a little more lined.

But otherwise Jonas Pettigrew looked just about the same —a hard-bitten rogue of the sea, who should have lived in the days of Morgan and Kidd, who would have been a fitting companion for the notorious Bully Hayes, but who, nevertheless, was doing his best to emulate his more illustrious predecessors.

But what did fill Tinker with a sense of relief was the fact that he could detect not the slightest sign of recognition in Pettigrew's eyes. After all, they had only come actually face to face some years before, when Tinker had been younger and considerably less developed physically than now. Also, that meeting had been during a wild melee on board the Eastern Queen, so it was not strange that Pettigrew should not recognise him. But he had noticed by now that the young man who stood before him was not the one he had engaged as wireless operator the day before; so he frowned.

"Well, who are you?" he growled.

"I have taken Baxter's place, sir." answered Tinker civilly. "He went ashore last night on an errand, but just before he had been ashore long he had a bit of an accident, which made it impossible for him to sail. So I offered to take his place, and he accepted. I am a fully certificated operator, sir, and am fully conversant with all the duties. I should have reported last night, but did not wish to disturb you."

"Huh! Fully certificated, eh? What happened to Baxter?"

"Just what I said, sir —an accident. It was no fault of his."

"Blazin' funny that it should happen the very day he was engaged! Didn't seem as if he would skin out after getting the job. He was anxious enough for it. Wal, I guess if you know your job, young feller, you can fit in. Same pay; same conditions. You mess here if you wish, and the 'prentice relieves twice a day in spells of four hours. I guess that's all. Set in, if you want to, and hev breakfast."

"Thank you, sir! I had some coffee and rolls in my cabin. I will get back now and tune up. There is a little work to be done on the batteries. I'll fix up the hours with the apprentice afterwards."

Pettigrew nodded, and, after saluting again, Tinker turned and strode out smartly. It had been easier than he had anticipated, and as he passed Morales he noticed that the other scarcely glanced at him. He made his way back to the wireless-room, and put in a solid two hours' work going over his installation, for he had certainly told the truth when he said it needed attention.

Then he put on the phones once more, and was sitting thus when Blake's reply came through. As he read it Tinker grinned, for it was plain that Blake was annoyed. But he simply answered with the single word, "right," and let it go at that.

Several days passed without incident. Tinker managed to keep pretty well out of the way of Pettigrew and Morales; nevertheless, he had his eyes open constantly, in case some incident should occur which would either prove or disprove his suspicions. About the only person with whom he had any conversation was the apprentice, who relieved him twice a day. Tinker pumped this young man cautiously, but either the apprentice knew nothing, or was too well on guard, for Tinker got nothing out of him.

So it went until they were well past the Azores. And then one day his chance came.

Jonas Pettigrew may have been an unprincipled sea pirate, but he was, at the same time, an efficient skipper in both steam and sail. Therefore, when, after a bit of a blow off the Azores, it was reported that some of the cargo had shifted slightly, Pettigrew gave immediate orders that the forward hatch was to be taken off and the cargo re-stacked.

That was Tinker's opportunity, and he lost no time in taking advantage of it. He did not put in an appearance until the work was well under way, and then he strolled forward in a casual way, as if idly interested in what was going on. And he felt a sharp thrill run through him as, gazing down into the hold where the crew was at work, he saw tiers of long narrow cases, which might have contained "plantation implements," as stated on the manifesto but which might serve equally well for the packing of service rifles. And adjacent to these cases were several other tiers of what was, on the face of it, "whisky," for the cases were stamped with the name of a well-known brand. But Tinker opined that they might serve just as well for the packing of ammunition.

That night he made a tentative effort to get in touch with one of the stations on the American seaboard, but the atmospherics were either bad, or his sending radius too weak, for he raised nothing. Nor was he able to do so until two nights later.

On that occasion he managed to get through to Key West, and from there his message was relayed through to New York. It was that message which Bryant Kennedy showed Sexton Blake on the latter's arrival in the Bretonic.

And it is known how, from that on, Tinker kept in intermittent touch with Blake and Kennedy, as they dashed down the coast in the Revenue cutter.

But while Blake and Kennedy had been so puzzled and uneasy over the S.O.S. message, which had apparently come from the Belle of 'Frisco, and increased by the broken message which had followed it, there could have been no other ending to Tinker's adventure, considering what had transpired after the Belle had rounded Key West, and had started down the gulf.

It was then that both Morales and Pettigrew began to show signs of activity. It was then, too, as Blake had surmised, that while he was listening in the apprentice had heard the position of the Revenue cutter, as the station at Key West had given it broadcast. But Tinker was entirely unaware of that.

The apprentice had reported to Pettigrew in the usual way, and immediately after this Pettigrew and Morales had gone into conference, so to say. Both knew quite enough about the Revenue cutter, Mobile, to realise that if she was making down through the gulf she was either on some definite raiding effort, or was nosing about on general principles.

She had the reputation of being the hottest member of the fleet which made life uncomfortable for the rum-runners, and as the Belle of 'Frisco was, indeed, to be relieved of her cargo through one of the rum-running systems —just as Tinker at first, and then Blake, had surmised —it behoved Pettigrew to keep his ship clear of her.

It was then that the devious mind of Morales evolved a scheme which he thought would work. At any rate, it was decided to try it.

The scheme was very simple in its way, consisting, as it did, of a plan to lure the Mobile to a certain spot in the gulf by means of a fake S.O.S. signal, and then, while the Revenue cutter was searching the barren face of the waters for a ship that was not there, to run the cargo ashore north of Brownsville, in the state of Texas, and close to the Mexican line.

Once the contraband was ashore, the system there would find little difficulty in passing it along to the spot where Morales' agents would receive it, and run it across the Rio Grande into safety. It was almost exactly the scheme which Sexton Blake had figured Morales might try.

But Blake had not figured on a fake S.O.S. call.

Morales and Pettigrew both made their way to the wireless-room, where Morales drafted his message. Tossing it on the desk, he curtly bade Tinker to send it. While Tinker was reading the draft. Morales moved across to the table and sent out a few random signals on the key, but it was sufficient to show Tinker that the Mexican knew the code all right. He realised then that he was in a tight corner.

He could not imagine how Morales and Pettigrew had got to know that the Mobile was in those waters. He knew that he himself had not given the information away, and could only conclude that in some way the apprentice had received the information.

What was the object of this obviously fake message, he couldn't understand just then. He knew the position given was not the true one, and he knew, further, that the Belle was not in distress. His humble mind grasped, however, that for some reason Morales and Pettigrew wanted to bluff the Revenue cutter, and, with the pair standing there beside him, he could not very well refuse to send the message off.

Nor dared he change it in the sending, for he knew now that Morales would spot the trick at once. So he decided he would send it, and as soon as a chance occurred he would follow it with a correction.

One thing gave him satisfaction, and that was that Morales and Pettigrew could not possibly know that Blake and Kennedy were on board the cutter, which showed that it was the cutter that they feared for some reason, and not the two detectives who had been in daily touch with the wireless operator of the Belle.

So while he knew the message would cause some consternation on the Mobile, Tinker tapped it off in full. When he had finished Morales gave a grunt of satisfaction, and, turning to Pettigrew, said:

"I will draft out another message for our people ashore, so they will be sure to be on time. That point ten miles north of Brownsville will be the best. Mustn't try to land too close to the town, now that the Revenue cutter is dodging about. We'll make the coast this evening, and before the cutter finds out she has been fooled the stuff will be safe ashore. Then it won't matter if you are searched."

Pettigrew grunted an agreement, and the pair went out.

"So that's the game!" thought Tinker exultantly. "Ten miles north of Brownsville. I guess you are due for a slight shock, friend Morales. You will find the cutter has not been decoyed as you think. I'll just get our present position, and shoot it along to the guv'nor, then I'll tip him off that tonight's the night. You said more than you thought then, you crooked greaser!"

With that, Tinker strolled out of the wireless-room, and made his way to the bridge, where his presence created no comment. He idled about there until he was able to work his way into the chart-room, where the daily position was shown on the big chart which hung on the wall. Tinker took a swift look at this in order to get their position as at midday that day.

Then he made his way back to the wireless-room. On the way he took care to note that Morales was not on deck, for he realised now just how much risk he had been running all the time.

It had been sheer luck that Morales had not spotted him, and he might easily have done so, for until that day Tinker had no suspicion that the Mexican knew how to operate.

Once inside the wireless-room he seated himself at the table, and once more began calling the Mobile. He had little difficulty in getting her, and as soon as she had confirmed he began tapping out the message which would spoil Morales' little plan.

He was going strong, when a slight noise behind him —more vibration than actual noise —caused his hand to falter as he turned to see what it was.

He started to his feet as his gaze encountered the furious eyes of the Mexican. All too late, Tinker realised that the Mexican had probably just gone below to draft out the message he intended sending to his Confederates ashore, and that he must have returned to the wireless-room in time to comprehend some, at least, of the words Tinker was tapping out.

There was hot murder in the man's eyes, and as he jerked back his chair and came to his feet, Tinker sought desperately for some weapon with which to counter the attack which he saw coming.

But Morales gave him no time.

Before Tinker could even jerk off the phones, the Mexican gave a leap, at the same moment clawing out a heavy revolver. In the next instant he had reversed it, and Tinker was still trying to struggle free of the phones when the heavy butt crushed down upon his skull.

He went down as if he had been poleaxed, twisted convulsively once, then lay still.

Morales gave Tinker no time to defend himself. Before the lad could jerk
off the ear-phones, the Mexican leapt forward, clawing out a heavy revolver.
Reversing it, he threw himself on the wireless operator of the "Belle of
'Frisco!" (*Chapter* 7.)

HOW long he remained unconscious it was impossible for Tinker to guess; but that it had been for some hours was evident, for, as his senses slowly cleared and he lifted his head, he found himself lying on his bunk in the cabin adjoining the wireless-room.

A shaft of light came through the port from a flaming gasoline torch somewhere on deck. It was night, but whether early evening or early morning he had no means of knowing.

But what he did soon discover was that while his legs had been left free his wrists had been securely bound behind him. He discovered, too, an odd difference about the feel of the ship to which he had become so accustomed during the past ten days, and as his brain grew still clearer he found the explanation. The engines were stopped.

As that fact broke in upon him, he detected and listened to a new sound, and as he solved this puzzle the whole truth burst upon him.

The Belle had arrived at her rendezvous. The winches were working, which meant that the rum-runners' lightship must be alongside, taking on the cases of contraband.

In that case, what had become of the Mobile? Was she still scouring the empty waters in search of the Belle? Or had Blake sensed something wrong from the disjointed message which Tinker had sent, and in that case would his deductive faculties put him on the right track before it was too late?

If not, then Tinker realised that in his own condition of present helplessness the game was up so far as they were concerned.

Painfully he managed to wriggle himself off his bunk and staggered across to the port through which the light was coming. Craning his head there, he was able to make out that some sort of work was going on forward; but just what it was he couldn't see, although it was a pretty good guess that the contraband was being discharged.

But Tinker was not to be left for long in ignorance.

While he was still peering through the port he heard the door of the outer wireless-room slam, and a few moments later the door of his cabin was kicked open. Tinker turned to find that Pancho Morales had entered, accompanied by Jonas Pettigrew, who was carrying a lantern.

"So you've come round, hev ye?" snarled Pettigrew. "Well, me young bucko spy, stir yer humps! Yer agoin' on a nice long ride, and when yer gits ter the end uv it yer'll do no more spyin' in this world. I've spotted yer now, and the seenyor here has a few things ter say ter yer. Come on!"

With that, while Morales stood grinning, Pettigrew grasped Tinker by the shoulder and shoved him heavily towards the door. He drove him into the wireless-room with a well-placed kick, and then the lad was hustled out and along the deck towards a ladder which had been thrown over the side. Despite the pressure from behind, Tinker managed to pause before going over the side. He took a hasty glimpse seawards, and for a brief instant he thought he saw the flash of a distant searchlight.

Then, as his gaze swung back, he made out a glow to the south which he thought possibly might be Brownsville. Then just beneath him he saw a large motor-launch, piled high with cases which had been taken out of the still open hold of the Belle. On the night air came the sound of other motor-engines, and straight ahead he could see several lights on a darkly-lined shore.

It was plain, even in that brief scrutiny, that the whole of the contraband cargo had been got out, and that the boat by which he was to be taken ashore was the last one to go. A feeling of futile bitterness welled up in the lad as he realised that all his efforts had gone for nought, and his feelings were not salved by the ironical reflection that there was a good chance that the distant searchlight might be that of the Mobile.

He was pushed over the side and assisted down the ladder.

He knew there was nothing to gain by putting up a resistance, so beyond kicking a Mexican rum-runner in the jaw as he slumped aboard the launch, he obeyed instructions.

Morales followed him at once, and even as the launch drew away Tinker heard Pettigrew giving orders for the hatches to be replaced. The Yankee apparently intended losing no time in getting outside the three-mile limit, where he would be safe.

It was less than half a mile to the shore, and as the launch nosed into the soft sand Tinker was unceremoniously dragged out and dumped on the beach. He was left there for some minutes while a score or more of what he made out under the light of several lanterns to be Mexicans unloaded the contraband. They made quick work of it, and as soon as it was finished the launch pushed off and went at high speed in the direction of Brownsville. One certainly had to admit that the rum-runners had a well-organised system.

Then Tinker was dragged to his feet by a couple of Mexicans, and pushed up the beach to a sandy road, where he saw a fleet of no less than seven motor-lorries standing loaded and ready to make a dash for the border. He was bundled into the last of these, and dumped down in a narrow space between two piles of cases, while a Mex. dropped the tail-curtain and took up his place just inside.

"You, gringo, you mak' one leetle move an' I plug you full of lead!" he promised.

"All right, you dirty greaser; you've got me safe while I am tied!" snarled Tinker.

For answer the other jammed a heel into Tinker's stomach, in return for which the lad twisted round and drove out his heel, catching the greaser full in the chest.

The impact sent the Mex. out under the tail-curtain, where he landed on the ground to the accompaniment of a string of vile curses. The rumpus brought Morales along in a rage to know what the noise was about, but before the Mex could air his grievance Tinker called out:

"I'm your prisoner, but if that dirty greaser touches me again I'll kick him through that curtain every time he shows his nose."

Morales gave a grunt and struck the Mex. a heavy blow.

"Fool!" he rasped. "Do you want to be heard? Get in there, and guard that prisoner and keep quiet!"

The greaser climbed back into the lorry, taking good care to keep out of reach of Tinker's heels. Then the flap was dropped, the lantern disappeared, and there reached Tinker's ears the sound of the engines being started. He was able to make out first one, then another and another and another of the lorries starting off, until the one in which he lay gave a lurch and began to move.

"The whole outfit is off." he thought. "Pretty slick work at that, I must say. This bird, Morales, certainly knows how to organise his supply column. But he isn't over the border yet, and until he is I am safe enough. He won't dare play any hanky-panky with me until he gets me on his own soil, and while there's life there's hope."

He lay quiet then for some time while the lorry lurched its way along the rough, sandy road. It was impossible for Tinker to tell in what direction they were travelling, or at what speed; but he figured they had been on the move perhaps ten or twelve minutes, when suddenly there came a shout from somewhere in front.

Following that, the lorry in which he lay came to a jerking stop, and the next moment a perfect pandemonium broke out.

The man who was guarding Tinker rolled out under the flap, and as he reached the ground Tinker heard him give vent to a soft curse.

Then a wild fusillade of shots rang out, and, as if that had been a signal, the night became hideous with rapid firing, shouts, yells, and curses in vile Mexican, interspersed now and then by the curt command of voices having a different timbre. As a bullet tore its way through the canvas side of the lorry and plumped into a case close to Tinker, the lad began to try and edge his way along towards the end.

"If a few more like that come through something is going to start if it strikes the right spot in one of those cases of ammunition. I guess this is no place for me, but I'd like to know what is going on.

"It is a pretty warm scrap, from the sound of it, and it looks as if there was a hitch somewhere in Morales' plans. Darn this rope, anyway. If I could only get my hands free I'd be able to make it."

At that moment another bullet whistled past his head, and, with a grunt of annoyance, he dropped back into his place. He lay still, listening to the battle which was raging outside, trying to make out from the medley of sounds just what was going on. But so confused was it all, that beyond feeling fairly certain that some preventive men had raided the contraband convoy he could tell nothing.

By now the pandemonium had increased until the racket was deafening. If Tinker could only have looked outside he would have found his guess confirmed, for as the convoy had turned out of the sandy beach road into a wider road they had been held up by a well-armed posse of Revenue men who had rushed out from Brownsville.

But Tinker did not know that; nor did he know that the posse had been organised by a wireless message which had been sent from the Revenue cutter, Mobile, to the station at Key West, and then relayed on there by the land wires to Brownsville. Nor did he know that this was the result of Sexton Blake's going into action after the receipt of that broken message from the Belle.

All that afternoon, and during the evening, had the Mobile been dashing south towards Brownsville, for both Blake and Kennedy had agreed that the S.O.S. from the Belle must be a fake, and that it had been sent to lure the Mobile away from where the actual running ashore of the contraband was to take place.

How well they had figured can be seen by the fact that the Mobile had reached Brownsville at about the same moment that the Belle had started to discharge her cargo, and that even as the contraband was being piled into the lorries —six cars full of determined men were rushing out from Brownsville to cut them off. And if Tinker had been able to look out to sea as well he would have noticed a brilliant searchlight playing on the old Belle of 'Frisco, which was driving along as fast as her rickety old engines could drive her, trying to make the three-mile limit before the Mobile sent a shot across her bows.

But she was fated never to reach her goal, for a heavy "boom" which Tinker heard was the shot that was to bring the old hooker into the grip of the law at last, and was destined as well to curtail the activities of Jonus Pettigrew for several years to come.

Coincident with the shot from the Mobile, the pandemonium outside seemed to lessen materially, and after a few more scattered shots a comparative silence fell. Tinker lost no time in taking advantage of it. He had no idea which way the victory had gone, but he was determined at all costs to get outside and see what was afoot.

So, raising his voice, he began to create a yowling rumpus of his own that caused the few Mexicans who were jammed up against the lorry with their hands in the air to shiver in superstitious fear. But Tinker gained his end, for a few seconds later the tail-curtain was jerked up and a lantern flashed in his face.

"What the devil is all this row?" asked a voice, in strong American accent.

"Pull me out of here and I'll tell you!" answered Tinker. "My hands are tied and I can't manage it!"

"Well, I'll be —" began the other; but at that moment he was thrust aside, and a strong voice called out:

"Is that you, Tinker?"

"Guv'nor!" yelled Tinker. "Sure, it's me! How did you get here?"

"How did you get here would be more to the point," responded Blake. "Wait a minute until I get hold of your feet! That's it! Now, come along!"

With that Blake pulled him clear, and as Tinker dropped to the sand Blake took out his knife and slashed his bonds.

"Are you all right?" he asked quickly.

Tinker nodded.

"Morales nearly brained me," he said; "but outside of that I am all right. But how did you get here? How did you know where to come? What has happened?"

"We have made a clean sweep. I will tell you the rest after. Come along! Morales is riddled in half a dozen different places. Can't last long, and I want to question him while he is conscious."

The American preventive man grinned, but made no comment as Tinker stumbled along after Blake. As they passed the line of lorries Tinker saw the Revenue men securing their prisoners, while half a dozen lay sprawled out on the ground. None of whom would never run the gauntlet again in this life.

Blake had spoken truly. It had been a clean sweep, and not only had all the contraband arms been captured, but in the same action one of the most powerful of the rum-running gangs on the Texas coast had been smashed to pieces.

The Revenue men were highly jubilant, and no wonder.

Morales was lying at one side of the road, and as Blake bent over him Tinker saw that the bandit's minutes were numbered. He was still conscious, however, and as Blake spoke to him he opened his eyes.

"Listen, Morales!" said Blake quietly. "You are done for. You can't last long, and you are too badly wounded to be taken into Brownsville. I am giving it to you straight, because I believe you would prefer it that way."

The other nodded weakly.

"Si, senor; eet ees bettaire so."

"I want you to answer me a question, Morales," went on Blake.

"Who are you, senor?"

"I am the Senor Sexton Blake, of London."

Morales began to laugh in a queer, choking way.

Even at the point of death he could find amusement in Blake's words.

"So you are ze Senor Blake," he said, as he paused through sheer weakness. "Eet is ver' fonny, senor. I neffaire know you are here."

"Where is Senor Barbosa's daughter?"

Again that queer, almost soundless laugh.

"Ze Senorita Barbosa; you zay, senor. W'ere is the little man?"

"In Brownsville. He is ill there. He is suffering very much on account of his daughter."

"An' you say I die ver' soon. Ver' well, senor, you 'ave beat me. I tell you w'at you wish to know. The Senorita Barbosa, she eez quite saf'. She is marry."

"Married! Did you marry her, Morales?"

"No. Leesten. I die ver' soon. Car-r-ramba, it not mattaire now. The senorita is senorita no longer. She eez the Senora Morales, but not ze wife of me, Pancho Morales. I tell you. You 'ear many fonny tales of Pancho Morales. You 'ear, per'aps, zat he eez more zan human, because he mak' it posseeble to be in two place at one time. You hear zat? Yes?"

"Yes, I have heard that."

"I tell you. Me, Pancho Morales, I 'ave ze twin brozzer, Ricardo. Ricardo 'e is not ze rebel. E eez ze quiet man who nevaire fight. Bueno, senor. I steal ze leetle senorita, but before I can marry 'er, my brozzer Ricardo he hear of what I do an' he com' to me. 'E love me ver' much, an' I lov' eem ver' much. He say me, I must not 'arm ze senorita, but give to 'eem. So I say all right, my brozzer, you tak'. So 'e take, and 'e marry. They both ver' happy because Ricardo eez ver' good man. You tell little Barbosa eef 'e go to Alamos he find both. They write many lettaire for to find Barbosa, but I stop zem all and destroy because I 'ate Barbosa. Zat eez all, Senor Blake.

"But eet eez ver' funny. I not 'ate you, senor, for w'at you do, but no more Pancho Morales 'e fight for Mexico. Eef I haf' be ze president of Mexico, I, stop all ze fighting long ago. But eet ees too late now. Eet eez ver' fonny how I die. I —ah! —por dios, senor — por dios —zees —zees eet ees ze deat! W'at you zay —adios —por dios —por dios —"

And as his voice drifted off into a thin whisper, Pancho Morales fell back in Blake's arms. He had spoken truly —he would never fight again.

Blake eased his head down gently, and removed his hat.

By now Bryant Kennedy had come up, and several of the Revenue men were gathered round that scene of death, and not one of them but agreed with Sexton Blake when he said gravely:

"Poor Morales. He was a great man in many ways. If he had been on the side of right instead of wrong he might have indeed have reached the president's chair. And, who knows —he might have been the one strong man poor Mexico needs. But he chose the other path, and here he lies dead, an outcast on the sands of a barren coast. But he deserves no small meed of forgiveness for the atonement he has made this night."

There is little more to tell.

Blake, Tinker and Bryant Kennedy accompanied the Revenue men, their prisoners and the dead, back to Brownsville, whither the Mobile had convoyed the captured Belle of 'Frisco. There Blake told Senor Barbosa of Morales' confession, and, when he had finished, the joy exhibited by the poor old man was pathetic to behold. Nothing would do but he must start off at once for Mariposa, from where he would be able to cross over to Alamos.

Blake arranged matters so he could do so, and after promising to let Blake know at the first opportunity what the result was, he drove off.

One thing Morales' confession revealed to Blake was how the wily bandit had taken advantage of the likeness his twin brother had borne to him to allow the wild tales to grow and spread until the ignorant peons had come really to believe that Pancho Morales was some sort of superman, and that he actually could materialise himself in two places at the same time.

As for Blake, Kennedy, and Tinker, they elected to return to New York by rail; and the following day, after making a formal statement to the authorities, they got away.

In New York, just before sailing, Blake received a long cablegram from Ricardo Morales, in which he told Blake that Barbosa had found them; that his daughter was now completely happy, and that it would be his personal care to see that the old man was restored to the state of comfort he had enjoyed before his brother had ruined him.

"So you see, you did leave London and settle the old man's affairs after all," remarked Tinker slyly as he and Blake paced the deck of the liner after bidding good-bye to Kennedy.

"For the simple reason that you went off like a reckless young ass, and forced me to cross the Atlantic," answered Blake with a frown. "And you can take it from me, young man, that you'll keep your nose good and close to the desk when we get back to Baker Street, until you have made up for lost time."

Which threat didn't worry Tinker in the least.

He knew the chances were that by the time they did get back to Baker Street it might be necessary for them to plunge immediately into another case. And at that he wasn't very far wrong.

THE END.
[22600 WORDS]

Back Numbers for Sale—

U. J. Nos. 979 to date, except No. 994: 2d. each, plus postage.—W. E. Maw, 88, Argyle Street, Leicester.

U. J. 30 misc. Nos. 963 —1,019; 3s. 6d. the lot; separate numbers 1½ d. each. Good condition but football coupons missing. —Albert Lloyd, Merthyr Mawr, Brigend, Wales.

U. J. Nos. 930 —1,020; complete with supplements from 939; good condition. Also about 45 misc. Nos. of Nelson Lee Lib. and S. B. Lib.— Arthur Artless. 31, St. Bartholomew's Terrace, Church Hill, Wednesbury, S. Staffs.

Det. Mag. Supp. Nos. l—12. 14—52; either singly or the lot. — E. Beck, 13, Cambridge Street, Millom, Cumberland.

U. J. misc. Nos. between 960—083, and 985 to date. —Offers to H. E. Tebby, 726, Chester Road, Stretford, Manchester.

U. J. misc. Nos. 891 to date, 1d. each. Misc. Nos. S. B. Lib. to date, 2d. each. Write for list. Postage extra. — G. Crocker, Netherleigh, Somerville Road. Sutton Coldfield.

U. J. Nos. 886—1,024. Write offer. —H. Simmons. 23, Evering Road, Stoke Newington, London. N. 16.

U. J. Nos. 900 to date, minus supplement, at 1½d. each, post paid. Also 200 other boys' papers.—Write Kevin O'Farrel, 44, Laurence Street, Drogheda, Ireland.

U. J. misc. Nos. at half-price — Write W. Smith, 2. Brickfield Terrace, Norwich Road, Attleborough.

U. J. Nos. 1,016—1,021. Perfect cond. —Write Thomas Keogh, 75, Summer Hill, Dublin.

U. J. Nos. from Sept. to date. Also a few S. B. Libs. —Write, enclosing stamped envelope, to C. J. Lofmark, 120, Taybridge Road, Clapham Common, S.W. 11.

U. J. Nos. 905—1,099, and 1,001— 1,021, less supplement, at 2d. each. — Write John Wilson, 10, Primrose Street. Leith, Scotland.

U. J. misc. from No. 946 to date. Good cond. —Write A. Elliot, Grove Hall, Retford. Notts.

U. J. Nos. 940—1,020. Write offer. —C. New, 6, Philip Street, Back Church Lane, St. George's, E. 1.

Printed in Great Britain
by Amazon

38178210R00040